"You're not looking for me, are you?"

He jumped, and his forehead banged against the pillar. The voice from behind his shoulder startled him. Toby slipped away from the wall, and faltered two steps before regaining his balance. Losing his footing, he would have landed on the floor had he not grabbed the corner of the column. He regained his stance, embarrassment at being caught flamed before he was able to stand tall. Pulling at the hem, he adjusted his shirt back into place.

In her gold and sand-colored vest uniform with the beige skirt and matching low heels, she was even more striking than in her runners and baggy sweat clothes. She lifted a hand to hide her well-formed mouth, covering her snickers. Her eyes sparkled, the edges crinkled with mirth.

Praise for Lori Power

"Set in the iconic Hotel del Coronado, reading this book is like taking a vacation. This story is full of twists and turns that captivate the reader. Sea Breeze (book one in the series) is a wonderful book filled with characters that come alive."

~Margaret Marlow

From the Front Desk

by

Lori Power

The Gentle Surf, Book Two

From the Front Desk

Cover Art by *RJ Morris*

The Wild Rose Press, Inc.
PO Box 708
Adams Basin, NY 14410-0708
Visit us at www.thewildrosepress.com

Publishing History
First Champagne Rose Edition, 2017
Print ISBN 978-1-5092-1797-7
Digital ISBN 978-1-5092-1798-4

The Gentle Surf, Book Two
Published in the United States of America

Dedication

Thanks to the "Tragically Hip" for their inspiration.
"Rock On!"
~*~
To my dad
for instilling the love of books and stories
and being ever vigilant
in your support of my writing

Chapter One

Sweat dripped from the ends of Wendee's short hair. The light brown strands appeared almost black with the accumulated moisture where they flopped in front of her eyes, in rhythm to her step. She huffed and swiped the curtain of bangs back from her brow. The dribble oozed its way along the edge of her ear, creating a tickle she couldn't ignore. She scratched the side of her neck, then rubbed the moisture on the cotton shorts without breaking stride. Her sneakers slapped the sidewalk, the sound a musical accompaniment to the bass-thumping pop song blasting through the earbuds. She relished the freedom of running outside. Even at six in the morning, the California coastal island of Coronado was hot compared to what she was used to in the Midwest, and the sun hadn't broken over the horizon yet. Fortunately, by the time the sun reached its summit, she'd be surrounded in air-conditioned luxury.

At home, this time of year, all activity seemed to center around hockey and hot coffee. As she imagined the caffeine boost, she poked her tongue out to run along her lips. Soon. For now, she tasted only the salt of her efforts.

Minnesota. Not her home anymore. Roger had seen to that. A quell of fear, like smoke from a fire, burned as she thought of him.

Wendee slowed her speed near the entrance for the

special forces, Sea, Air and Land—SEAL—training base. One of three on the island. Could there be a safer spot in America than the island of Coronado? Her fingers crossed in superstitious hope that this was, indeed, the case, and her bravery returned. Someone at the front desk at the Hotel Del Coronado had told her how many military installations were present between here and San Diego, but she'd forgotten. She'd have to ask Eva. Suffice to say, more than a handful. Would the location provide enough of a deterrent?

Slowing, she tapped the light pole in front of the guard station, tag fashion. The air, heavy with humidity, took some extra effort to fill her lungs. Not waiting to see the officer, Wendee turned and retraced her steps along the residential road now busy with military personnel heading to work. The beach flanked her right, shadowed in the early morning, compared to the dark mass of the ocean beyond. Still, every few paces the scent of sunscreen permeated her nose. Beautiful houses followed the road along her other side. The A-frame, Cape Cod-style beach homes left her in little doubt to the enormity of their worth. Thanks to family connections, in her present lodgings, she could safely say they were as beautiful on the inside as they were on the outside.

She rubbed her chin along the shoulder of her T-shirt to clear the drip and winced. The bruises were slow to heal.

The electronic voice from the running application on her smartphone updated speed and distance. She had reached the halfway mark. She squinted, blinking hard, and increased her pace.

The song in the playlist spoke of freedom and

taking chances. She nodded, trying to convince herself she, too, could be that kind of person. She'd been lucky. Evangeline Vincent, a cousin from the banking end of the family, welcomed Wendee with few queries.

The girls had been pen pals when they were children, retaining a connection digitally rather than physically. When, in desperation, Wendee sought the help of her cousin, she'd half expected to be turned away. But, to her relief, the bond was well forged and strong between the two. Astute beyond her age, which was within months of Wendee, Eva seemed to understand her and didn't press for more. The longer the time they spent together, Wendee knew a kindred spirit and a true friend in Eva. With this new friendship, she felt the strength of independence flow through her blood.

Wendee shot a look to the sky to gauge the time. Like a blister on her heel, thoughts of Roger returned. Surely, he'd be glad she'd disappeared and leave it like that. Even if he were interested, under the circumstances, it seemed unlikely he would find her. But she didn't want to assume. She'd made that mistake more than once and ended up at the ass-end of that statement. For sure, he blamed her for a lot of the shit that went down, never believing she knew nothing of the location of the money. She was just the bookkeeper...she ran her fingers through her soaked hair and flung away the sweat before sprinting down the sidewalk. She had to let the whole misadventure go and move on. There was no turning back. She couldn't change what was.

She glanced to the horizon. Move forward. Nan would say bright futures lay ahead.

Her grandmother, Maribel Cavanaugh-Wakefield, was the best person Wendee had ever known. Likely the only one who would miss her, at any rate. Contriving a way to contact the care home after she fled had been an activity in imagination. Not that Nan would necessarily know Wendee was missing most days, but she did have some lucid times. Early onset dementia made her more susceptible to emotional outbursts than she had been. The last thing Wendee wanted was another reason for Nan to be upset and wonder where she went. For all these years, they'd been each other's only family.

Landing the position at the front desk more than a month ago offered the perfect solution. Twice now, she'd sent postcards she purchased from gas stations while driving here. No return address. The notes were always simple, but cryptic, providing enough information to let Nan know she was okay. The simplicity of sending the cards seemed inspired. Comfortable with her position, Wendee would engage the hotel guests in conversation, hand them a card with a buck for postage, and ask them to mail it from their hometown.

"My nan likes to collect stamps postmarked from various locations." Here she would shrug. "Something she started as a hobby when she was a little girl and had pen pals. Of course, I can't travel everywhere, but since you're from…" It really didn't matter where the guest was from, just so long as the town was outside the state of California.

The two she'd sent so far were greeted with smiles and, "Isn't that a marvel idea?" One commented that she, too, may do that for her grandmother. "She's in a home now and can't travel at all. Imagine how much she would like to get mail." Wendee nodded in agreement, and the pleasant conversation had continued until a new customer arrived.

The roar of a helicopter over the bay interrupted her thoughts. Wendee glanced around before crossing the intersection. She loved the island, as she could never have imagined taking to a place so quickly. Friendly people with a real sense of community, yet she was able to keep to herself without worrying about causing suspicion. She shrugged, wondering at the winding road that was life. Who'd have guessed a meandering bridge, a marvel of engineering skill, would intrigue her enough to cross to the other side, both literally and figuratively, only to find a home when she landed on a relative's doorstep?

Diverging from the sidewalk, Wendee bounded down the small flight of wooden stairs to the pathway separating the beach from the resort-style hotel. Yes, stepping outside her typical character, she had taken a chance in contacting Eva, but, unlike other decisions that had kept her close to home, she had no regret.

This island offered a sense of tranquility—a pull and Wendee felt she could make her own way here. New life. The place was ageless and as cherished as a prized antique. The iconic red roof had attracted visitors for more than a century, yet she had never heard of it before Eva suggested applying for a position.

Contrary to the main road, on the boardwalk only a handful of people were out this time of the morning. The fresh sea salt air brought a sense of rejuvenation and hope, a feeling that had become so foreign she thought she had lost the capability. Another watchtower loomed ahead, the second angle in the triad of military bases on the island. Getting comfortable with her routine, she hoped to use some of her earnings to rent a bike for the afternoon and explore farther afield. Driving slowly through residential streets in a car—especially her old jalopy—would raise more than a few antennae. She glanced at the two guards at their post, curbed the urge to wink, and snickered at the thought.

The entrance to the military annex, with the twelve-foot walls, contrasted sharply with the beachfront where it met at the end of the boardwalk. However, the message was clear—no civilians past this point. Typically, Wendee would again tag the light post—a mirror to the one on the other end of the island—and go back to the other side, not yet familiar enough with the island to venture along the unknown streets and find the third base. But not today.

She had watched other runners move across the sand and run beside the breaking water. So today, feeling more courageous, she stepped off the path and crossed the sand to the beach to jog at the edge of the surf. Unlike the boardwalk, here the golden turf was hard packed, perfect for running. The joy of lengthening her strides and racing with the wind, watching water play with the shore, renewed her energy. Where she should be tired and slowing to a walk, she ran harder. The sun cast a merry glow from the left. Ahead, across a stretch of ocean, the land mass of Mexico materialized like a purple shadow emerging from the blue-green of the ocean, ahead, on the right.

All around, the sand shimmered like golden dust in the growing light. Blindingly white against the tan, a sand dollar. The tide crept forward to bathe the treasure and entice it back to its ocean home. Almost toppling with the discovery, she stopped, picked up the delicate shell, and ran a fingertip over the skeletal embossing. Here the briny smell from the fishing boats wafted stronger. Breathing hard, she straightened. Sea treasures. She cradled the prize in her palm and searched the horizon. Stretching her gaze across the vista, the last flicker of stars faded from view. The music from her headphones matched the scenery. The artist sang of new beginnings and, for the first time, Wendee believed this could be true.

Following the shoreline north to south, fishing rigs and patrol boats alike shared the seascape. She stroked the sand dollar nestled in her hand. Yes, this could be home.

A large hand tapped her shoulder, and Wendee jumped around, almost dropping the shell. Her heart thudded, and the breath whooshed out from the depths of her lungs. She folded her fingers around the fossil and held it to her breast before training her focus on the intrusion.

A sweat-stained, burgundy vee T-shirt filled her view. She ran her gaze up over broad shoulders, across a squared jaw roughened with light bristles reflecting the early sunshine, to the most stunning silver-gray eyes. Framed by dark lashes and lighter, sun-bleached straight brows, they crinkled at the edge as he peered back.

The intruder's reddened face glittered with perspiration. Over his ears, wet, honey-toned curls stuck out from beneath a bandana. His mouth, curved into a smile, opened and closed, yet she heard nothing. Those razor-sharp eyes seemed to sparkle with merriment, softening the effect, and his brows rose in a crinkle.

Wendee shrugged a shoulder higher to brush the edge of her shirt over her cheek and wipe some perspiration, suddenly conscious of her appearance. Her stomach clenched at his proximity. "What?" her voice croaked, sticking halfway up her windpipe. She coughed and struggled to hear what he was saying.

His lips, well formed and etched perfectly within the growth of day-old beard, moved, but still she heard nothing. The song, playing through the buds, drowned out anything he said. The lyrics spoke of a lover's caress, and she could easily imagine those lips finding the perfect places along her body in dire need of some attention. She shook her head to clear the inappropriate thoughts of a stranger, and sweat rained from the movement. She could smell her own exertion. Embarrassed, she stole a look at her feet, wanting nothing more but to shuffle away, take a shower, and meet him when she appeared and smelled significantly better than right now. The scents of seaweed and suntan lotion mixed with their odors to further enhance her discomfort.

Mesmerized, she watched his hand, with its long, tapered fingers, move toward her head. She rolled back her shoulder from his approach, and he smiled, flicked his fingers, and her earbud fell out.

"Oh."

His smile activated inch-long dimples in his cheeks.

Her knees tingled with a funny little tickle. A blush rushed up her neck and flooded her cheeks. Glad for the exertion from exercise to mask this, her gaze flicked from his face to his shoulders and back again.

"You better get going." He pointed a thumb over his shoulder.

The casual ease of his shrug held her enthralled, unable to respond. *Get going? Why?* Was he some sort of trainer? How did he know she needed to continue her run?

Getting a grip and remembering her independence, Wendee decided not to be bossed around. As though doused with cold water, she shrugged, opting to dismiss him and turn back toward the sea, but again his gaze captivated her and she stood staring.

Squinting, his gaze moving into the middle distance, he scratched the back of his head and adjusted the bandana. Then he drew a breath, which stretched his shirt across his chest. He lifted his chin a fraction in the same direction as his thumb. "You ought to get going."

The short sleeves bunched over his biceps, and Wendee couldn't see past the broad shoulders. The stranger stood at least a foot taller, so whatever interested him over there was his business. What she did notice, directly in her line of sight, were the pectoral muscles that stretched the thin cotton shirt and the sweat stains leading like a neon sign to regions south. She forced her gaze back to his penetrating silvery eyes. Remembering her pledge for independence and taking a grip on the distraction he caused, she retrieved the earbud where it swung loose below her chest. Before corking it back in her ear, she tilted her head and smiled. "Thanks, mate. I'll get going in my own good time."

The dimples deepened when he grinned down at her. With an unhurried movement, he pulled the rag from his head and wiped his face. The loose curls drifted like clouds settling. He retied the bandana and those sharp-colored eyes gave her the once-over. He glanced again over his shoulder and shrugged. "Suit yourself, then."

With the casual grace of an animal of prey, he turned and his long legs carried him toward the Del.

The loose blue shorts hung down to his lower thighs, but curved nicely against his backside, revealing sculpted buttocks. It cost nothing to look. But then, she twisted fully, curious to the direction of his interest. What had gripped his attention inland? Over the dunes, positioned out of reach of the breakwater and tidal pulls, black-clad SEAL training teams swarmed like ants leaving the nest. In teams of eight—four each side of a dingy—they were making for the water. Sand spat from their heels. Everywhere she looked, drill squads descended. Within minutes, she'd be swarmed and completely in their way.

Abandoning her poetic ponderings of new beginnings inspired by the discovery of the seashell, Wendee secured the earbud and in the same motion, her feet took flight. As fast as she could, she followed Mr. Well-Made's tracks. Though he quickly outpaced her and she lost sight of him in the distance, she kept going, not pausing or losing stride until she again reached the wide boardwalk. Once there, breathing heavily, Wendee bent from the waist and turned back to see the beach awash with military personnel deep into exercise maneuvers. In the short amount of time she'd been on the island, the one thing she had heard—and heard often—SEALs take their training very seriously.

Squinting into the distance opposite, she saw no

sign of the stranger. Likely a good thing. No one to bear further witness to her embarrassment. Looking down at her garb, she winced. She didn't go in for the fancy running gear. Her gym shorts were paint splattered, stains of better memories. Ripped in several places, the loose garment hung to her knees. Normally, she didn't care about such things—until she did—when a well-made man stopped to chat. No, she corrected, to warn her to get out of the way. What an impression she must have made. She picked up the edge of her T-shirt, plagued with the gray sickness and brown spots...maybe she'd invest in a better shirt if she knew she would meet up with lightning-eyes again.

"Puh," she breathed and dropped the shirt. "Whatever."

Casting one last glance around, confirming he was nowhere in sight, she resumed her usual pace. Wendee finished her run and walked back to her cousin's beautiful beach home, which had been in the family— her side, at least, since the fifties—all the while keeping an eye out for the handsome stranger. What did she care, anyway?

But, despite herself, she did.

Chapter Two

Toby sprinted down the beach, back toward the barracks. His arms and legs pumped in rhythmic unison, while his feet flung sand in his wake. Every once in a while, a clump thumped against his calves and backside, allowing small grains to leach inside his shoes. The acceleration of motion released endorphins, giving him an out-of-body high where he imagine he was somehow along for the ride on a more powerful machine. Then, just as he considered this, connection to his limbs returned and the burn rushed along his muscles, forcing him to slow his pace.

He shook his head, spraying sweat, and muttered a curse. Why hadn't he run past the woman? Why stop to assist some random female? So what if she was going to be surrounded by military maneuvers? Surely, on this island, the navy could handle inquisitive tourists. Not his problem.

Walking with his hands braced on either hip, fingers pressing under his ribcage, Toby slowed his breathing. Deliberately, he moved air in through his nose and out through his mouth. For years, like his exercise regime, he had conditioned himself and accepted a solitary life. He didn't *do* spontaneity. Not anymore. Experience showed impulsiveness was hazardous to his freedom. And random interactions with women daydreaming on the seashore didn't factor into his plans. Still, he couldn't figure such an impetuous action.

Safely away from the training beach, he stopped and stared over the vast expanse of ocean. The variations of blue, from indigo to violet, to the lightening of the skyline, filled him with a sense of contentment and helped to further calm him. He drank in the smell of fish and seaweed washed in on the tide. Saltwater ran in his veins. His mother always said so. Though he grew up along the cold northern shores of the same ocean, the warm southern Pacific offered comfort and conjured memories of his family and home.

If his mother were here now, with a twinkle in her eye, she would say the devil made him do it. And she'd be right. The briny vista filled his vision, but all he could see was his mother's smile, the deep dimple on the left side of her lower lip, and her strong chin. He remembered how she pushed her glasses into place, up the bridge of her nose, whenever she laughed. He grinned, reminiscent of times gone by when he teased her with a wink.

He lifted one arm and wiped perspiration from his brow with the back of his hand. Toby shook his head to clear the memories. Another life.

Walking toward the shore, he paused, stepping away from the breakwater to slump down on the beach and watch the sun crest the horizon. He trailed his fingers through the sand. The Del was just visible, to the south. The resort didn't maintain this area, so the beach remained rustic. He glanced at his palm filled with small pebbles. This lack of perfection made him enjoy this space even more. Natural, without man-made machine interference, just the way Mother Nature intended.

A trawler skimmed along the tide, reminding him of when he first arrived on the island. What a journey that had been. He was supposed to have swum to the Mexican shore. But during a storm in the middle of a moonless night, not knowing the difference, he pitched up on the US side of the border. Toby tossed the small stones back into the water and rubbed his palms to loosen the last of the grains from the crevices between his fingers. He leaned forward and laid his forearms on top of his knees. This location was more dangerous by far, but such was fate.

Here, by the touristy lighthouse, on a boulevard decorated with antique-style lamps, was his special spot. A reminder of a time he must never forget or ever openly acknowledge. Only he knew he had been reborn on this beach.

Amber eyes and flushed skin squeezed his heart and awakened something better left dormant. He ran a forefinger along his lips and pictured hers. What would a kiss feel like?

He curled his fingers into a tight grip and dropped his fist to the beach. "Shit," he huffed. Toby squeezed his eyes shut and scrubbed the cuffs of his hands across his brow. For the love of his mother and all she sacrificed—for all the times he took advantage and regretted his thoughtlessness—he should never have given in to the impulse of stopping for a girl. Well, she looked like a harmless girl until he approached and saw the woman with her curves concealed beneath floppy clothing. This morning, he broke his own rule. Never engage.

Yes, the devil made him do it. Not many people ran so early, even in southern California, so she stood out as a newbie. Seeing her pause along the beach and knowing she'd be swarmed by morning military maneuvers, he stopped. Her surprise at witnessing the SEALs training at the break of dawn confirmed his suspicions she was new to the island.

But, man, could she run. He had caught up with her when she leaped down the steps to the boardwalk. He admired her gait. Long legs stretching to full potential, eating up the distance, one with the wind. She loved to run, just like him. He could tell. Those who jogged for any other reason always looked stiff, their stride rigid, arms tight—forced to their sides. Those runners performed as though they were choreographed, manipulated, following some rulebook, and scared to break back into a natural fluidity. But not her.

He compared what he witnessed in her to how he felt about the sport. When Toby ran, he felt nothing but liberation, a sense that no one could catch him or stop him. No shackles. Every breath mattered. The soles of his feet connecting with the earth like a springboard propelling him forward.

Being able to run when he wanted, as far as he wanted, for as long as he wanted, was a freedom Toby would never take for granted. Not ever again. The manacles, once bound to wrists and ankles, still ached in a phantom memory. He glanced at his wrists where the faint white scars served as a reminder. He understood, all too well, what it meant when you couldn't run—couldn't take a piss without permission.

Toby wondered whether she, too, had run from something. *Nah.* There he was, letting his imagination get the better of him, as his ma would say. But the slope of her shoulders when she stopped to stare out over the ocean made him think of her as a lost soul—someone seeking peace—a kindred spirit—his sister. He shook his head and reached to scoop another fistful of the golden sand. He simply wanted to warn her. Normally, he'd be done with his run by the time the teams got to training, but he'd slept in. At any rate, he didn't want to see her overwhelmed when she clearly had no idea where she stopped to contemplate life, or whatever it was that had held her so fascinated in her own mind.

Sea birds screeched overhead. He glanced up at the lightening sky, watching them dive bomb into the water in search of food.

"Dammit, though," Toby whispered. He had broken the vow that held him fast these last years. Never engage. Yes, he could respond, but never engage. Never bring attention. That was the key to his existence—his very survival.

With a huff, he stood and scared the few birds milling along the beach back into flight. He brushed the grit from his backside and made his way to the sidewalk by the old lighthouse. Out of habit, he stooped to pick up multi-colored ocean-smoothed rocks along the way, clanking them in his palm as he walked. Again, his mother's voice echoed through his thoughts. "My dear Tobias, there'd never been a rule you didn't try to break," she'd say with a large grin and a hint of warning she'd never quite believed.

She'd been proud of him, despite himself.

He hadn't seen his mother, or his brother Robert in what seemed like a lifetime. Ten years today. A very long time. He'd like to think she'd still be proud. Toby tried to bring back his reminiscent smile, but he couldn't. The moment was lost and other memories—painful moments—filled his head. A period in his life he strove daily to thrust into a room he'd rather not explore again. Shoulders slumped, he looked down at his sneakers. Living through those times had been enough.

He used to tell himself the loneliness and longing for home and family would fade with time. His kin were better off thinking him dead. Drowned at sea in an attempted escape gone bad. He had caused them enough pain. By all accounts, he'd been but a child when he washed up on this beach, but time and growing into a man didn't lessen the pain of loss for a whole family, a way of life…

Yet, there was nothing he could do about it, so why dwell? He'd long since made his choices. He never had even tried to contact them. Constantly, he told himself they were better off thinking him gone forever. Now he simply had to live with these choices. He forced himself to square his shoulders and walk with purpose. Another lesson from Ma.

In the kinder moments, he'd tell himself in all likelihood Ma and Robert had long since grieved for him and laid his memory to rest, though Toby, himself, hadn't been able to forget about them. Nor would he want to. The memory of his family kept him going and made him strong. He constantly wondered about their wellbeing. Surely, if something had happened to his mother, he'd know…unlikely, but he told himself a certain number of lies every day. Didn't everyone? He wondered, as he walked, did Bobby ever marry that girl from prom? Was he a lawyer now, as he had dreamed?

Or was the loss of a brother and a sister within a year too much for a small, fatherless family to bear?

He didn't know, and sometimes the not knowing almost drove him mad with the wanting—the need to go back, just to find out and put his ghosts to rest.

"Ha." He shook the stones between his cupped hands, enjoying the music of their clanking together. There'd never be a going back. As she had given him life the first time, it had been his mother who granted him life the second time, as well. For once, he would do as he was told.

Slipping the pebbles into his pockets, he readjusted the bandana and took off down the trail, picking up the pace, shedding the irons of his memories, stretching his legs, and relishing the freedom of the always summer-like breeze coming off the ocean.

He cut through the parking lot of the Hotel del Coronado, hardly tossing a second glance at the magnificent fountain, making his way back along the road down to the marina and his houseboat. Thick foliage filled the air with pungent aromas of newly fertilized gardens. His nostrils flared, savoring the smells.

But then, as his mind relaxed again, his memory conjured the earthy fragrance of the woman. A mixture of exertion and simple perfume, combined with a hint of spearmint, likely toothpaste. Basic, real, and fragrant. A reminder of what he'd never had. A woman who glistened in the morning light from solid exercise.

He knew the route home without needing to pay attention to even the crevices in the sidewalk. His mind drifted, and the lush scenery faded. Soulful brown eyes filled his vision. Wide-set and round, her gaze held a sense of innocence, yet a knowledge of hurt. Loneliness? Maybe. Was he projecting? He didn't think so. In the small moment they shared, her confusion, her wonderment, filled him with a need to feel the arms of another wrap around his neck. To hold someone to him and relinquish his own isolation. And, to give comfort in return.

Yes, that was it. Like a magnet, when he touched her he sensed a deep need. A real longing—reminding him—of him.

Toby stopped suddenly and wobbled in his step. "Stop!" he hissed. "Just stop."

Chapter Three

Wendee scrunched her eyes then checked her watch before returning to the task of data entry. Three more hours and the shift would end. Her fingers hovered over the computer keys, and she contemplated the faint purplish scars. It seemed like she had made so many poor decisions with such drastic outcomes.

"Go big or stay home," Nan used to say when Wendee was young.

Who would have thought a candle placed so innocently on top of the fridge would have such dire consequences? She rubbed her thumb over the raised abrasion on the heel of her palm. She had forgotten to blow it out. Then the smoke alarm went off. By the time she ran from her bedroom, the top of the fridge was engulfed. Unthinking, Wendee seized the container and threw it into the sink, but residual wax spilled on the mat Nan kept on the floor and flame erupted just as Nan ran out with the fire extinguisher. Panic motivated her every action as she snatched the rug from the floor and tossed it outside while Nan pulled the pin on the extinguisher, but she couldn't reach the top of the refrigerator, being only five-feet tall, so Wendee grabbed a chair from the table, scooped up the canister and put out the last of the flames before the ceiling caught.

She didn't see her grandmother fall. Didn't notice

her hit the edge of the table on the way to the floor. All she registered was turning around and, in addition to the wax and yellowed powder from the flame retardant, an abundance of blood running from Nan's unconscious form.

Wendee blinked back the tears and folded her hands into fists. The doctors said she'd already been diagnosed with early-onset Alzheimer's but hadn't wanted to worry Wendee until she could come up with a plan, and the fall simply accelerated things along. But Wendee knew her grandmother well, and felt had she not suffered a massive head injury, they would have had a few more years together.

"Poor Nan," Wendee murmured and ran a finger under her eyes, gathering any moisture before it could be seen or, worse yet, commented upon.

"What?" said Calvin Hobb, her desk mate.

Wendee shot him a glance, confused. "Umm, what?"

"You said something."

She shook her head. "Oh, did I?" She nodded toward her monitor and splayed her fingers over the keys, turning her attention back to the work at hand. "Just reading what I have to type."

After a while, she noticed hotel maintenance conferred across the lobby foyer, drawing her attention from the computer screen. The staff needed to fix the broken elevator box—some of the indicator lights weren't operating and guests were complaining. Turning to Calvin, Wendee raised her brows and questioned whether four fellows were required for the job. "It doesn't look like they're doing anything to fix the elevator."

"Probably not even broken."

Wendee gestured across the foyer. "Well, obviously it's not working so it must be broken."

"Likely the ghost of the beautiful Kate Morgan," Calvin whispered close to her ear, his breath a mixture of coffee and a mint.

Wendee bit her lip to keep the squelch inside. "What? Who?" she squeaked, and turned her head in his direction. Her hand clamped across her heart.

"Oh, come on. You've worked here how long now? Close to two months," he returned coyly, answering his own question. He stepped back to his end of the reception desk, beside his computer, and pushed his tiny square glasses up the bridge of his nose with the knuckle of his forefinger. His perfectly symmetrical features glowed with merriment from his coppery complexion. "You can't work here even more than a week and not know the story of our most famous ghost."

"There's more than one?" She rolled her eyes, grateful for the distraction from her morbid thoughts of earlier.

Calvin's brows rose to hide behind the thick fringe of his cleverly styled hair, and he smiled with a nod.

Swiping the back of her hand across her forehead, regaining her own composure, Wendee turned to him, a hand on her hip. Thoughts of ghosts didn't bother her. In her opinion, the living provided more to fear than the dead. When she left the Midwest, she had only the vaguest notions of destination, more set on escape than relocation. Yet her grandmother, Maribel, had spoken fondly of the island, always with a romantic lilt to her voice and soon, in mind of Eva and the historical family home, Wendee found herself mapping her way to Coronado.

Nan's beloved brother, Reginald, and his wife, Elleah, had met on the island, at this very hotel in 1950. Evangeline Vincent, their granddaughter, settled in the seaside cottage the pair purchased after their marriage, always coming back to the island on their anniversary. Wendee stifled a laugh each time she walked into what looked to her as a mansion and have it referred to as a cottage. She could have fit the house she and Nan shared into the two-story A-frame three times over.

Ironically, her grandmother also credited the resort with her own freedom. "Reginald came away from there a changed man and rescued me."

Her grandmother had been institutionalized by her father—Declan Cavanaugh, millionaire banker and a man of position in New York society—for a scandalous affair with a married man, which resulted in the birth of Wendee's mother, Alexis. Reginald saw to the release of Maribel by the year's end, where she was reunited with her daughter to live a quiet life in Minnesota.

Wendee blinked several times to clear her focus. She searched Calvin's face for signs of trickery. "Tell me," she said, hoping to encourage the story without seeming too eager. Besides, she welcomed the chatter over the churning of her thoughts, which kept racing back to things she couldn't change. "Just who is this fabled ghost, Kate Morgan? And don't tell me she's related to the sea captain."

Calvin edged closer and chuckled as a breeze whistled through the lobby lifting the hair off her brow and raising gooseflesh along her arms.

"Surely not," he said. "Though, perhaps a dose of

the good Captain's rum may have steadied the ol' girl and she wouldn't be so fond of haunting our halls."

To curb the sudden shiver that raced along her spine, Wendee smirked and folded her arms across her chest, preparing to listen.

"In 1892, a beautiful young woman checked in alone. The unusual occurrence of a woman travelling unaccompanied caught the attention of the staff." Calvin, in full story mode, illustrated lively with his hands, his face animated with revelry, his dark eyes almost black, eclipsed by his pupils. "Diaries of staff members here at the time recount how Miss Morgan seemed to wither physically from one day to the next, muttering to herself. Then"—he paused dramatically— "within four days of wandering the various hallways and grounds, she was found dead on the stairs outside the hotel after one of the most violent storms in memory."

Wendee dropped her arms to her sides. Her palms faced the heavens. "You're kidding? How'd she die? In the storm?"

"No." Calvin leaned forward in an exaggerated posture from his waist. He positioned two fingers, curved his thumb, and pointed the imaginary gun. "Bullet." He splayed his fingers wide.

"Suicide?" A tingle raced along her arms, leaving her hair standing on end in its wake. She imagined Roger's contorted features while he stood above her, loaded gun in hand, blaming her for the missing money. Wendee shook her head, returning her focus to Calvin. "Or was she murdered?" Had it not been for the police sirens creating a momentary distraction where she was able to get away from Roger's iron grip…Wendee pictured herself on those steps…

Calvin shrugged. "No one knows. The gun was found beside her." He stepped closer still. "But here's the rub…she was never properly identified. No one ever came looking for her, and no one knows if Kate Morgan was even her real name."

"And she haunts this place?" Wendee was unconvinced, though she deliberately ignored the hair standing straight on her arms.

Calvin lifted his chin and pointed a thumb to the elevator across the foyer. "Shit like that happens all the time. Working great one minute, then, poof, broken." He put both hands together then splayed them apart to mimic an explosion.

Wendee laughed and turned back to the computer, determined to forget the story and Kate Morgan as soon as her shift ended. "So you say."

"So I know," he shot back. "Even after a century, no one really knows why she checked in…or checked out the way she did. Nothing in her belongings gave rise to her true identity, and she remains the 'Beautiful Stranger' of the hotel to this day."

"So you say," she repeated, shrugging to rid herself of wayward thoughts Calvin's story conjured of Roger and another of her fateful mistakes.

"You'll find out, my lovely girl," he shot back, two fingers aimed like a gun toward the computer monitor before resuming his position at his end of the counter. "Every week, without fail, someone comes to the front desk complaining about flickering lights or curtains blowing when the windows are closed. Hell, the historical society even sells books in the gift store on her."

"I guess I'll have to get myself a copy." Wendee wasn't looking forward to having to explain away ghostly adventures to guests. It was one thing to deal with real concerns like the noise of clanking tools, rowdy occupants, clearing accounts for check-outs, and preparing for the arrivals rush after lunch—quite another to have to explain away the supernatural. By the afternoon, Wendee was counting the minutes. Fixing the broken elevator was now the big issue, because the guests complained the workers were in the way. She'd smiled her way through enough explanations for one day, her jaw hurt.

"Seems like a no-win situation, sometimes," Wendee mumbled to Calvin's narrow back when he returned from his break and walked toward his end of the desk. "Whether they want it fixed or not."

He faced her with a large-tooth grin. "I know, right?" he said, and straightened his bowtie. "I lost the business card for the magic fairy hotline. Of course, all their fluttering would get in the way, and likely one the guests would think the pixies were bugs and squish them."

"Better pixies than ghosts, though." Hand across her mouth, Wendee snorted in an attempt to conceal her laugher as a client approached the front desk.

"I'm sorry," the gray-haired man said. "But I really must know the weather forecast for the weekend. The almanac suggested a clear, dry spell, but those clouds out there leave me wondering if I should be ordering tents for my daughter's wedding."

Assuming the father of the bride wasn't from the San Diego area, or the coast, for that matter, where weather changed at the whimsy of ocean current,

Wendee gathered herself from the fit of giggles and concentrated on his obvious distress. She pointed to the forecast monitor to the right of the counter and easily visible. "This television is always tuned to the weather network." She modulated her tones into soothing comfort as she read the verbiage that appeared on the screen.

The man's features relaxed, and his shoulders lowered from his ears. "Oh, that is good to hear. Thank you so much. Such a relief." He consulted his phone.

Wendee nodded as the man turned to the bank of elevators.

Then he pivoted, cell in hand, thumb poised on the face. The worried frown returned to his heavily lined face, deepening the creases between his bushy gray brows. "But just how long will those men will be hanging around the elevators? The problem really should be fixed by now. They've been there all afternoon."

Calvin started a low, moaning keen from across the length of the desk, and Wendee did all she could to ignore him.

"As I understand it, sir, they ran into some complications with the wiring—"

At that moment, a worker's toolbox clanged shut. Up on her toes, she peered over the gentleman's shoulder. "There now, you must be good luck." She lifted her chin in indication of the area directly across the foyer. "All done, no issues at all."

The man slapped the marble top. "Good job," he said and all but clicked his heels as he sprang away.

Wendee turned to Calvin. "I guess the lovely Kate has had her fun for the day."

Calvin adjusted his glasses and rolled his eyes. "You'll see."

A little later, Wendee retrieved a stack of receipts for the auditor from the main floor café, but her gaze veered longingly toward the front entrance and the sunshine beyond. Bright blue sky edged the top of the colored glass, and she was reminded of her encounter this morning. Strange. Which encounter caused the greater flush, she wasn't sure: the man, or the quadrant coming over the dunes? How mortifying to be caught standing there in a trance while the army performed maneuvers.

Both. Equally.

Then a deeper heat dropped to her core as she recalled those silvery eyes smiling down at her. Would she see him again on her next run? While the sane part of her brain told her to steer clear, the less-than-modulated part of her brain had already planned what time she needed to leave on her run in the morning to "chance" another encounter.

You'd think, with the problems she ran away from, she'd steer clear of any entanglement, but did that mean she had sworn off men? A sense of freedom rushed her nerve endings. For the last few years, she had taken no time to even meet a man of interest, let alone allow herself to indulge in fantasies of meeting a stranger on a beach. A bit of fun didn't mean entanglement. Continuing the conversation in her head, she argued though she had no desire to enter into another disaster, she knew most men were not like Roger—well, at least she hoped not, and their relationship had never entered the romantic zone. Hell, she didn't think she'd gone beyond apprehensive until their last encounter where she fully embraced petrified.

Heart pounding, she shook her head and forced her attention to the tasks at hand. Returning to input reservations, she huffed when she typed "silver" where she should have put "Springer" as the guest's last name. Her fingers stalled on the keyboard, and she lifted the top page of the list to regain her focus. Instead of the words, she saw damp curls sneaking out from under a soaked bandana, and she rolled up on her toes.

For heaven's sake. Their meeting, if it could be called a meeting—encounter—had been but a few moments. How could she possibly recall so much about some random stranger? Perhaps his ruddy complexion highlighted the lightness of his eyes? The soft glow of the rising sun accentuating the reddish golden stubble across his jaw. How much distance did he clock today? Did he run every day?

"Stop."

"What?" Calvin cast her a searching gaze.

Feeling the hair on her head prickle with the force of being caught yet again talking to herself, Wendee mumbled, "Nothing." She fished through the drawer to her left to rifle some reservation cards. "I think I misfiled one of the cards."

"Need some help with that?"

"No, it's all good." She shook her head and looked across to the bank of elevators where the crew had been only moments before. The area had been swept clean, and she marveled at the efficiency of the hotel staff. Everything they did was for the client experience. As Susan, their stately front-desk supervisor, said, every smile mattered. Of course, these witticisms were always followed by some absurd comment like, "Count your blessings you don't have to sleep with them."

What did that have to do with anything? Sex seemed like a distant memory at this point, and random encounters didn't constitute a relationship.

Was that what she was looking for?

Certainly not now.

Frustrated, she cast her gaze across the foyer, searching for focus. A tall man in a white smock crossed the carpeted area by the large, ornate grandfather clock. She recognized him and her heart ticked an extra beat. Light curly hair tied at the nape of his neck highlighted high cheekbones. No doubt. Right there, casually striding through the hotel, was her random encounter. The man from the beach. His long legs carried him gracefully through the lobby where he turned a corner into the spa boutique.

"Who was that?" she asked breathlessly before she could halt the words.

"What?" Calvin's chin lifted from his chest where he had been concentrating on the computer. He adjusted his glasses and braced his palms on the marble to peer over the counter. "Who?"

"Too late," she said, hearing the remorse in her voice. "He's gone."

"Now I'm interested," Calvin said, smoothing out his eyebrows. With a wide smile, he stacked the paperwork into a neat pile and thumped it into order. "I'm done for today, at any rate. What'd I miss?"

"Just some guy."

"It's never 'just some guy' when a girl's eyes go all round like that and glisten like a mirror."

Wendee shrugged and smiled. "I thought I recognized someone, but he disappeared into the spa, and I'm sure this guy would never be in the spa." She had an image of the typical female spa workers who concentrated their efforts on nails and hair. This lithe male with wide shoulders and powerful biceps didn't fit within that mold.

"I wouldn't be too sure on that. There's always Tobias, who stands outside any stereotype you may have imagined for working in a spa." Calvin whistled a soft inflection. "Yes, Mr. Tobias MacPherson."

A shiver shot from behind her knees to course up over her body. She resisted the urge to fluff her hair. Instead she dropped her hands to her sides. Wendee turned to Calvin, palm up, arched her brows, and left the question unasked.

Calvin grinned, hand on hip, the fingers of his other fanning his face. "One of the masseurs from downstairs. If only he were *my* type."

She stepped back a pace, unsure how to respond. "What?"

Calvin flapped a hand. "Never mind. I don't know what *his* type is, to be honest. I've been here more than three years...he's worked here even longer, and I tell you no one's ever seen him with anyone...male or female. Such a shame, and not for lack of trying."

"You hit on him?"

"Good lord, no. A quick conversation confirmed he wasn't for me." Calvin lifted the edges of his bowtie and lowered his lids into a sleepy gaze to regard her through his exceptionally long lashes. "But, honey, I'm just sayin', I'm not sure he's for anyone. Except for that hair, I'd put him on the Monk list."

A challenge had always intrigued her. Nan's voice echoed through her memory, reminding her those kinds of rash reactions were the same that had gotten her mother in trouble. Wendee closed her eyes and bit the inside of her cheek. Now, of all times, was really not the occasion for such frivolity. "Umm, interesting," Wendee said, the siren warning system of her grandmother's voice being switched to silent. Maybe she needed a distraction. Feigning disinterest, Wendee resumed her work, all the time imagining mussing those curly locks of one Mr. Tobias.

Chapter Four

Right or wrong, history proved Wendee always could talk herself into anything. After her fleeting glimpse of the man from the beach—Tobias—in the hotel lobby, Wendee fantasized over how she could somehow stumble into him again. That night she laid out her best running clothes, which is to say, they were frayed rather than ripped. The next morning, up at five as usual, she retraced her route, even veering off the boardwalk to run along the shoreline. However, on alert and aware she had limited time before the SEALs converged on the beach as the sun crested the dunes and she heard the assembly of the troops, she gave up and ran home.

The mist, which had started to fall on her return journey, turned to drizzle, and then an outright downpour. Grumpy over her foolishness and soaked, Wendee arrived for her shift less than enthusiastic.

If attitude is everything, it was no wonder everything she touched and everyone she encountered seemed just as cranky. The rash of check-outs slowed to a snail's pace when the computer system broke. The bellmen vanished, leaving the guests wondering after their luggage. The valet "bumped" another vehicle, leaving her alone covering the desk while Calvin handled the insurance, and Susan soothed the guests.

"Kate Morgan's at it again," Calvin muttered,

portable phone in one hand while he strode to the back office.

Having just mollified a guest complaining about the weather when they had planned to spend the day at the zoo, Wendee shrugged, in no mood to play. "How can the ghost of Kate Morgan control the weather?"

Calvin paused at her tone, one brow raised. "Not the weather, pet, the luggage, the fender bender, you name it. She's on one of her rants."

"Yeah?"

"Yeah." He nodded, and the bland echoes of spectrio on-hold music wafted from the handset. "Whenever the gales froth the sea and the rain teem down the same as the night she died, havoc breaks out here."

Wendee pinched the bridge of her nose. "Very poetic. Maybe the sun will come out, and we can get back to work."

A voice sounded from the phone and it was Calvin's turn to shrug. "Suit yourself." He rounded the corner out of sight.

Wendee focused on the monitor, fingers poised over the keyboard, willing the machine to return to normal functioning so she could start on the growing pile of paperwork already completed by hand to get through the rush. She inhaled a deep breath, held it for two heartbeats, and released it on a whoosh. She stared up at the ceiling and drew air deep into her lungs.

"Hey." The gruff voice caused her to start and stare at the handsome face creased with frustration. He rapped his knuckles on the marble. "Earth to clerk."

"Yes, sir, how can I help you?" Wendee forced her features into a smile, determined to prove Calvin wrong and redeem the remainder of the day.

Deep brown eyes blazed back. A sardonic twist curved his full lips. "Thanks to the less-than-competent service this morning from your hotel, I'm now running late for my flight, and I have to take a cab."

"I'm sorry to hear that, sir," she replied automatically, bracing herself for another mollifying session. "We are doing the best we can. It just seems to be one of those days."

"One of those days?" he echoed, his brow furrowed, and he slapped his palm flat on the desktop, his weak chin disappeared into neck. "What would you know about one of those days, other than fluffing your hair and showing up?"

Wendee had learned to cope with frustrated customers; they could be mean and hateful at times with their words. Still, the man's handsome face had become quite ugly. His tanned features had, within moments, burned to a deep puce. "I didn't mean to insinuate—"

"Miles."

"Pardon?"

"My name is Mr. Miles."

"Well, Mr. Miles, I didn't mean to excuse the lack of service this morning, only to—"

"Make more excuses? Umm." His arm had stretched across the width of the marble top so his fingers curled around the edge closest to Wendee. "If I don't get back for my meeting this afternoon, I run the risk of losing out on a deal worth more than your annual salary." His stare raked her from head to toe. "Likely two years."

She resisted the urge to step back, drew another

breath, and started again. "How can I help—"

"Call me a cab and return the rental car." He slammed the key ring with the fob on the desk with his other hand. "Check me out, and do your damned job, for once."

"I'm sorry, sir—"

"Mr. Miles," he barked. "My name is Mr. Miles. Use it so I know you will get something right today, and I won't be paying for someone else's room in addition to everything else."

"Mr. Miles," Wendee enunciated every syllable and pulled on the reins of her temper, aware of the customers queueing up behind and not wanting to make more of a scene. "I will make sure you are checked out correctly and call you a cab; however, I cannot—"

"You see." He pointed a finger directly into her face, almost touching her chin. "That is exactly what I told you not to do." His voice had risen, and a woman behind him gasped. "Now," he said, after a brief pause, his lips lifted to reveal straight teeth, and he winked. "I asked you to return my rental car so I can get to the airport without further delay, and you're gonna be a good girl and do as I say."

A good girl? Did she hear him correctly? "As you say—"

"As I say," he said, slapping his hands together to end with his palms facing her and backing away. "Finally."

"I didn't rent the vehicle. You did," Wendee said, tensing up on her toes to lean in to the desk, bridging the newly formed gap. "You didn't rent the car from us and, as I don't even know who the rental agency was, I can't possibly return it."

"You will." He pointed to the keys lying untouched close to her hand. "I'm leaving." He turned then and started to stride away.

Wendee grabbed the keys in one hand and called, "Mr. Miles." She bounded up, reaching as far across the divide as she could, and called again, her tone like honey melting. "Mr. Miles, sir."

He stopped midstride and turned back to look at her. "What?" he shouted.

Heart hammering, Wendee teetered the fob between her finger and thumb until they generated a slight tinkle. "See these?"

His gaze narrowed, but he didn't say anything.

"Not my problem," Wendee said, heat flaming her cheeks. Cupping the keys in her fist, she pulled her arm back and tossed them across the lobby where they landed perfectly in the trashcan with a noisy clatter. Then she bounced back to her perch, straightened her vest, and greeted the next guest with a wide grin. "How can I help you?" she said, striving to get her breathing under control.

The couple stared but hesitated to step forward.

Wendee held up her palms. "It's okay—"

"The hell it is." Mr. Miles had returned to shove himself ahead of the elderly couple. "You're gonna—"

"Perhaps I can help you." A deep voice resonated above the clatter, the calm cutting through the chaos.

"And who the hell are you?"

"Tobias MacPherson."

"She"—Mr. Miles pointed a thumb over his shoulder at Wendee—"just threw my keys away."

"I think, Mr. Miles," Tobias steered the angry man away from the desk, across the foyer toward the trashcan. "We can retrieve your keys, have the valet gather your car straight away, and get you off to the airport."

"As I told that stupid girl—"

Wendee watched a muscle clench in Tobias' jaw. "Mr. Miles," there was a warning note in his tone. "Let's avoid a discussion of intelligence at this juncture and get your keys then get you back to making money."

Bending swiftly, Tobias reached into the can and straightened, the keys dangling with a slight tinkle. He handed them to Mr. Miles, then ushered him to the entrance and had a quick word with the valet.

Within moments, a car appeared, and Mr. Miles was gone.

At that moment, Wendee's computer monitor blinked to life, and she released the breath she had been holding. Aware of the customers, she pulled her focus back to her work. Her fingers trembled, and she gazed beyond the sea of faces, across the foyer, to the side of the trashcan, and could have sworn she saw the flash of a misty white dress take the corner, out of sight.

Chapter Five

As he did daily, Toby rolled over on his bunk prior to the alarm buzzing and laid a hand flat on the side table. After a misspent youth of never being able to get up on time, now he seldom slept past five. With his other arm over his head, he stretched, wiggled his toes loose of the sheet, and waited for the singsong start of the clock's signal. He didn't know why he didn't just turn off the device when he woke. But, then again, he liked the routine and the reminder that he was able to choose when he would rise and sleep, not someone else.

Water lapped along the side of the houseboat, and the gentle sway eased him into the day as he laid his bare feet on the planked floorboards. It would be a while yet before the dawn, but he loved to run when the streets were quiet and the dew lay heavy on the manicured lawns. The temporary housesitting arrangement meant he need not be listed as homeowner, renter, or resident. The fact that *temporary* had stretched to close to a decade didn't seem to draw any attention.

When poor ol' Jack had died without any family to stake a claim, Toby felt little guilt in assuming the costs of mooring. People didn't ask, and he didn't tell. Just the way he liked it.

His hand swung loose between his knees. He gazed at the knuckles of his left hand and rubbed a forefinger over the purplish scar. What had started as a means of his father to toughen him up had turned into a competitive sport for Toby, then the means of his ultimate arrest when his hands were considered a weapon.

Toby lifted his hands to run through his hair. *Stupid girl.* The words reverberated through his skull as he remembered the itch he'd had to lambast the arrogant son-of-a-bitch. "Shit," he muttered, knowing he had to put her out of his thoughts. But she worked in his hotel.

Toby shook his head to clear the thoughts and stood as tall as he could in the confined space. He arched his back relishing the snap of the vertebra, and stretched his fingers across the wood-lined ceiling. Feeling the vigor surge through his veins at the beginning of a new day, he bent to grab running gear from the shelf. After he dressed, he filled the water bottle, tucking it inside the pouch at his waist, and prepared to leave.

His thoughts shifted to the chance encounter on the beach, followed by seeing her, eyes flashing, behind the front desk. Her defiance and verve propelled him forward to take action. He thought she had a handle on the situation until she tossed the keys in the trash, and he saw the switch in Mr. Miles. Toby knew then that a man like Miles relished humiliation. Toby couldn't stand by and watch. He had to step in.

Toby walked across the decking and onto the dock, wondering if he would see her again. Did he want to?

Yes.

It wasn't the first time, out of sheer curiosity, Toby had approached a woman who, for one reason or another, reminded him of his sister, Carrie. Perhaps the way she stood, the sway of her short hair, even the manner of speech, and each offering its own disappointments. There would never be, could never be, another Carrie. His beloved dead sister was never coming back. He had to live with that knowledge every day. Especially the part he had played.

This time though, with this woman, it was more than the reminder of a long-lost sister. A fire blazed in the depths of her eyes that he felt, rather than saw, from even across the lobby of the hotel. An electricity which attracted him. Yes, Carrie had that kind of zest, the ability to stand tall in the face of adversity, but she had been his sibling. This was a woman who blazed a path without even knowing she was doing so.

Toby stretched a leg behind him then switched, feeling the pull on his calves and thighs. He bounced up on his toes, then rolled back on his heels. He squinted down the road, through the darkness, allowing himself to reflect on the memories that flowed freely.

Carrie had been older than he by a mere ten months, but she acted as though the age difference was far more significant. His mother used to say Carrie was born thirty-five. She had been both his closest confidante and the biggest pain in his ass.

Until she wasn't.

He took off at a trot across the sway of the dock, up the stairs two at a time, until he passed through the gate and to the hill. The bark of a dog in the distance broke the bedded-down silence of the early morning. The streetlights glowed a hazy yellow in the morning fog. Head bowed with concentrated effort, Toby climbed the steep slope, picking his speed as he advanced the crest.

He sprinted down Ocean toward the hotel, crossing the parking lot until the lane turned onto the boardwalk and the vista of the Pacific came into view. In the distance stood the SEAL tower, and he sped toward it.

When he slowed his speed yesterday, he had been intrigued—captivated really—by the way her expression reflected such peace. A grace he craved. Her skin a healthy glow next to the blue-green sea with the morning dawning behind her. The whimsical stance, her hair spiked upon her crown like a pixie, holding a shell in her palm, she gave him every impression of his having discovered a fairy, and he had no choice but to stop. Then, as he came near, and her tawny eyes stroked him without actually seeing him, he had been filled with a joy that bubbled up from a depth long forgotten. Of course, now he couldn't shake her from his mind. The memory of that moment. And that was trouble.

Separating his needs from his wants had always been easy—in theory, if not in practice—but he wouldn't lie to himself. He definitely wanted to see the woman with the round, startled eyes again. He wanted to see her high color glow almost crimson with surprise. He wanted to ignite the spark he had seen yesterday at the front desk. He was a man, however much he had denied himself, and she had triggered an electrical charge, a current he couldn't deny.

Blurred lines often got Toby into trouble when he was younger, though he had done an admirable job these last years of keeping his distance from such vices. His job as a masseur had aided in this endeavor. Using his hands to heal rather than wound. With considerable effort, at the hotel, he had created an air of aloofness, a persona non-committal to either sex. He declined offers from men in the same manner he declined the women, striving to never give away too much. Revealing even a little could cost him everything.

His steps thumped against the boards as he ran past the miniature lighthouse. Daily, he passed the spot and always lifted a prayer of thanks for ol' Jack Carson.

Toby had washed ashore grateful to be alive. Unsure where he was in the world, and unwilling to venture far for fear of being caught, he had stayed close to the lighthouse, scrounging for food left from picnickers. Jack had been a fisherman, long in the tooth, alone in the world. When ol' Jack found him on the beach, near starved and at a loss as to what to do next, Jack took him in—no question. There had been an understanding in Jack, as though he had been in Toby's shoes at one time. Like a father, Jack brought Toby back from the brink, saw that he got a job, arranged for him to be educated, and then, just as Toby settled into his position and place on the island, ol' Jack took his last breath with a smile on his wrinkled face.

Angry with himself and this preoccupation, he ramped up the music volume to his earbuds to drown his treacherous thoughts and focus his concentration. The maneuver was a temporary respite, at best. By mile five, the sweat-soaked bandana couldn't hold back the rivulets of moisture coursing down his brow and over his cheeks. Breathing heavily, he brushed fingers across his eyes, clearing the sting of salt. He rounded the back residential streets to cut across to the eastern side of the island, skirting the entrance to the naval yard. Turning south, he ran down the beach toward the SEAL training center. Those guys were tough. In another life…perhaps.

Rain or shine, cold or sweltering, the military specialists trained and trained hard. Toby wondered, if certain events never happened, would he have gone into the military? The attraction to their discipline and routine—camaraderie close to an obsession. Sometimes, he would watch them complete their maneuvers just to try to pick out some exercises he, too, could incorporate into his day. Many of his regular clients were spouses of soldiers and, with his expert touch, he would chase away the physical response to their emotional worry of the next mission. Sometimes they told him about the life of a person who had to always put their life secondary to duty and the greater good of the country. Toby wondered if he could achieve such selflessness.

Sprinting down the boardwalk, he leaped the stairwell and landed lightly onto the wooden walkway. The pathway meandered along the seaside, leading past the cottages, the hotel, and eventually to the SEAL beach. Gasping for air, he stopped just short of the hard-packed sand at the end of the route and fell to his knees to regain his breathing. He hadn't run that hard in a long time.

Sitting back, rear end on his heels, he grasped the stitch under his ribs. The seabirds, well awake, screeched, circling, looking for their breakfast of fresh fish and seafood. With the stars faded and the sky lightening in purple and rose hues, he knew if he waited, the platoons would start their daily drills. Heart rate resumed to normal, Toby got to his feet, walked a short distance across the sand, and picked a spot best for viewing. He pulled the bandana from his head and mopped his face with the damp cloth. He shook his head like a dog to release the loose drops clinging to the ends. Switching the playlist from hard rock to something more calming, Toby waited.

The soft breeze off the ocean cooled his skin, leaving a salty sheen. The tide was low. He might take a dunk before jogging back. He flapped the bandana against his raised knees and twirled the material, preparing to tie it back into place when a set of sneakers lodged in the sand next to him caught his eye. He flinched as he realized someone had perched down, and he hadn't noticed. His gaze travelled up the bare, lightly tanned, well-formed calves, over the knees to the frayed edge of gym shorts, then quickly to the familiar face.

She smiled widely, eyes crinkled with mirth and filled with warmth. Today, she wore a ball cap positioned low on her brow so her ears folded over the edge, resuming the pixie air. She reached to pull an earbud from its lodging, mimicking his actions of days before.

"I thought I might find you here." Her voice held a mild huskiness of being used for the first time that morning. She nodded as though confirming her suspicions. "Thanks for what you did yesterday."

Toby shrugged and opened his mouth to speak, but the words wouldn't come.

"I totally lost my shit," she continued and laughed. "That guy really got to me. Honestly, if you hadn't stepped in, I think I would have likely been fired."

He shook his head. Words wouldn't form. They started and lodged in his throat. He had thought of her so often, he almost considered she was a mirage brought on by lack of air when he ran. He lifted a hand to his forehead and flexed his thumb and forefinger across the ridge. The hotel?

He must have looked perplexed, because her brow wrinkled and she cast her gaze to her shoes, seeming unsure. "I work the front desk," she murmured, her voice losing some of its zest. "You stepped in to help with that Mr. Miles creep."

"Yeah." He coughed, dropping his elbows to his knees. "Yes. I remember…of course, I remember." He paused to stare, knowing her to be truly sitting beside him. "What an asshole."

Her laugh sounded relieved. "He really was." She scooped handfuls of sand, allowing the grains to slip between her fingers. "You work downstairs, right? In the spa?"

Was that a judgment? He wondered what the boys from home would think of his profession. Lifting his palm, he turned to gaze at her though he couldn't see any evidence of her being snide. He lowered his hand to the beach and drifted his fingers along the sand. He nodded.

Her smile filled her face, complete with dimples, and a mischievous sparkle lit her eyes, adding to her fairy-like appeal. "Good. That means I'll see you around."

His stomach almost tickled with feather-like sensations. His brain lacked proper function, and he wondered again if he had starved himself of air. Finally, after a much-too-long pause, a word brushed up over his dry windpipes. "Okay."

The lines to the edge of her eyes deepened, the smile lessening to allow her straight teeth to pull at the edge of her lower lip.

The gesture was so sexy he felt an instant arousal

and adjusted his seated position to cover.

Her gaze never left his as her tongue sneaked out to trace the contours of her bowed lips, and Toby ached to do the same—what would it be like to brush his tongue along the fullness of her lower lip? Her lashes fluttered like dark wings to complement her gentle brown eyes as she leaned closer and laid a palm against his cheek. Then, as though in answer to his wishes, she brushed her moistened lips across his. Feather light, but unrushed, and his heart stopped. She edged back just enough to look him the eye before leaning close again, laying a claim with her mouth as no woman had ever done before. She molded her lips to his as though they had been forged from the same iron and her tongue slipped between to reacquaint after a long separation. Yet, he had never known her before and somehow felt he had known her his whole life.

Though he hadn't moved, he responded, feeling her need piercing his own lonely longing for connection. If this was a dream, he didn't want to wake up.

She broke the kiss but kept her palms on his cheeks. "That was nice." Lowering her hands, she stood and brushed the sand from her backside. "See ya around."

With that, she turned and bounded across the sand toward the hotel, leaving Toby more breathless than when he had sprinted.

Chapter Six

Toby scrubbed his hands under the hot water. The sharp heat burned while he moved the thick lather in between crevasses. He scooped up the scrub brush and worked the bristles under his nails. The routine helped him focus. This girl—he didn't even know her name— had thrown him completely off his game—not that he ever had much of a game. From day one, when ol' Jack took him in, his plan had been limited to keeping himself to himself. There, he broke his own rule and now look.

He squeezed his eyes closed and flared his nostrils to breathe deeply of the thick aromatic botanical scents. The ambient music of garden insects and birds annoyed today rather than soothed. Normally, Toby relished the calm within the natural essence of the spa environment. Lush foliage complemented the shrubbery appeal with the waiting lounge opening into the actual garden complemented by fountains and stone walkways, entirely private from prying hotel guests and tourists alike. The gabled trees created a cathedral appeal where raised voices were never heard. Even in the treatment areas, the ceilings were adorned with silk grapevines twined in the open rafters.

A manicured hand curved around his forearm, drawing him from his musings. "Tobias?"

The perplexed squint and heightened color, told

him Scarlett had been trying to get his attention for a while.

"Umm, what?" Toby turned toward the small, brunette client in-take specialist.

Like the majority of the staff, she wore the light-patterned uniform. The oriental-style neckline and straight pants flattered her solid frame. Short but sturdy best described her. As the guest greeter with the fancy title, her uniform featured long sleeves, while practitioners, like Toby, wore short. The neatness of the outfit suited her tidy countenance.

Hardly seen without the tablet held in the crook of her forearm like a clipboard, Scarlett kept the spa operation running in a timely fashion with no one ever late or put off their schedule. However, at that moment, the forever-composed Scarlett let her work mask slip, and Toby saw a version of himself reflected in the depths of her light green eyes. Had she noticed his discomfort? How had he worked with most of these people for years and never taken the time to get to know them? So wrapped up in keeping to himself, he had managed to ignore those who surrounded him daily.

He nodded and smiled to let her know all was well.

Scarlett bowed her head over the tablet before returning her gaze to his. Her bright, red-lipped smile widened as she pulled back her hand to tap on the tablet in the crook of her other arm. "You were quite absorbed."

Reaching for one of the small plush towels, Toby dried his hands and turned to the linen basket to hide the heat flooding his face. "Just thinking."

"We're all entitled."

Toby craved a quick comeback, but Scarlett had stepped away, moving through the corridors ensuring everyone was on point and ready to service their clients. She had a knack for making each guest feel like they were their only customer—their number one, and he didn't know if anyone had ever thanked her for that monumental feat as it made their job so much easier. To please a client who was already made to feel special simply by walking through the doors was no effort at all compared to the opposite approach.

Calmer with thoughts in order and focused on the task to come, Toby followed Scarlett down the hall to the guest retreat lounge—a sheltered sanctuary. The thick, moist air gave an impression consistent of a tropical climate. Large-leafed potted plants and trees separated each area, creating the illusion of privacy for their guests from the other clientele. Fountains in each corner added to the humidity under the glass-domed roof, leaving Toby conscious of perspiration. The gurgle of water and muted conversations enhanced both the serenity and tranquility they strove to achieve. Cucumber and lemon-infused water, all-natural smoothies, fruits, and muffins were displayed artistically in the middle of the room.

He and Scarlett paused by the door, just out of sight. "A bridal party," she said, her voice hushed, gaze glued to the tablet screen. "Seven in all—two moms— the bride, of course, and the rest bridesmaids."

"Sounds like a fun way to start the day."

"The mother-in-law-to-be has a history of medical issues." Scarlet recounted a few of the highlights. "We think you better take her, but she's nervous about having a male masseur."

Used to the stereotype, he nodded and crossed his arms across his chest. Either she thought he was going to have his way with her, or he'd expose her to an altered sexuality, Toby thought as he peered around the door. Toby folded his fingers under his chin, used to how some people—males, mostly, and some older women in particular—were uncomfortable with a man in his profession. Touch created an intimate and emotional connection with another person. He never took his task lightly. "I'll talk to her first, then, shall I?"

"If you would." She nodded, her cropped curls wobbled in agreement. "I'll hold off bringing in any of the other specialists until she decides."

Having boxed for most of his youth, the guys he grew up—sparred—with would share some snickers if they knew what he had chosen as his profession. When he was a kid, there were loads of biases and interesting names for a man who would work in a spa, be a nurse, or even a dental assistant. Toby never envisioned himself as a masseuse. What started as a means of escape—hiding from anyone who happened to look— had become a passion. He reveled in his ability to use his hands to heal, rather than inflict pain. From the first moment he started to train, Toby felt an understanding of the body and the emotional power of connecting with another, even for just an hour. In this digital age of separation by one electronic screen or another, people seemed to crave the power of touch even more as a fleeting commodity.

Releasing his arms to fall to his sides, he pulled the hem to straighten his shirt around his hips. He confirmed there were no stains or water drops he may have missed. He loosened his hands, flexed his fingers, bunched them into fists, and finally relaxed his limbs and himself. In the moment, Toby stepped into the room. "Eliza Sharp," he called, without raising his voice. The deep tenor carried through the sultry environment.

"She's over here," chirped a giggling girl with eyes too big for her face. "Oh, man, looks like you're in for a treat, Eliza—*yum*."

A tall, raven-haired beauty escorted the older woman toward him. As she twirled a loosened tendril of hair around her fingers, her gaze raked him from head to toe. "Eye candy like you should be rented by the hour."

He half expected her to be chewing bubble gum. Suppressing a smile, he focused on the older woman. These comments ceased to embarrass Toby a long time ago. He didn't consider this a reflection of his looks, as much as the environment, the situation, and the presence of men in general being uncommon.

The older woman brushed a hand against her cheek and turned to the bold girl. She shooed her back to the crowd of peering women. "Excuse her. I guess her manners haven't woken up yet."

Toby flapped his hand in dismissal, leaned down marginally to bridge the height gap, and then laced his fingers together. A lack of reaction was the best weapon. "Do you mind if I call you Eliza?"

"No. No, of course not." Self-consciousness rolled off her in waves, and she pulled the robe around her plump body, striving to close the V over her ample bosom. "I'm not used to such a place." Her hand stole to her hair, smoothing the tendrils back into the bun at her nape.

He smiled and reached but paused mid-motion. "May I?"

Eliza seemed to ponder him with a skeptical twist to her penciled brows. But, with a quizzical lift to one, she placed her hand in his.

He lowered his voice, knowing the deep pitch could carry to boom across the room if he required it to. At this moment, though, all he wanted was to sooth and reassure. "Now, I want you to know." Toby placed his other palm on top of hers, so her hand was sandwiched between his large ones. "If you are not comfortable having a man for your therapy session, we have a lot of very capable and talented women to make your experience the best it can be. That's our job—to provide the best, most comfortable atmosphere...relaxed."

Eliza had vivid, light blue eyes. Weary lines etched from the corners. Her focus fluttered across his features like the scuttle of clouds. Color grew on her cheeks, and her eyes moistened slightly. Then, with a decisive nod, she said with a small smile of forced bravado, "I'll bet not one of them can hold a candle to you."

Toby nodded and couldn't disguise his grin. All his concentration focused on Eliza. "I'm sure they could, but I'd never tell them," he said with a wink, leaning in as though to share a secret. "I'd never get that raise I've been vying for."

Eliza's face lit then, and age washed away. He slipped her hand in the crook of his arm and escorted her to the treatment room.

Introducing her to the salon and leaving her to be settled, he returned in moment, seeming unhurried, but keeping to the schedule to have her choose her scents and where she would like him to center his efforts. Eliza had experienced a ripped rotator cuff years before and, though she'd had an operation, the shoulder continued to give her pain. After a bit of discussion, he gained permission to work the pressure points, and see if he could provide some relief. Older skin exhibited less elasticity, so he used the pads of his fingers to probe. Sighs escaped and a visible release of tension from the cords of her neck made him smile. Gently, he worked the shoulder, maneuvering the arm, closing his eyes, imagining the muscles and tendons beneath the skin as he worked.

By the time she rolled onto her back and Toby threaded his fingers into the more pliable muscles. Pain relief did that to a person. A relaxing technique, he spoke soothingly about some easy exercises she could do to keep the area agile.

When he escorted her back to the sanctuary, she turned at the entrance. Taking both of his hands, mirroring his actions of their initial meeting, she smiled. "Thank you."

With a full roster, clients provided a necessary distraction. On break between appointments in mid-afternoon, Toby's curiosity got the better of him. Taking the employee stairwell, he strode into the hotel lobby. He slowed on the carpeted hallway leading to the foyer as he considered what he would say to her—this mystery woman who'd kissed him like a long-lost lover on the beach. He couldn't say he didn't enjoy it. Nor would he say he didn't want to enjoy a kiss, though common sense cautioned him against such thoughts.

Stomach clenched, Toby paused before turning the corner to where the front desk sat dead center of the hotel main floor. He swallowed the lump lodged in his throat and flexed his shoulders under the fitted smock. He'd walked these floors many times, yet now, everything felt different. He was again the stranger, seeking. Within the order he had created where all he had to worry about was himself, now, a woman filled his focus.

And why? Because, since he first saw her, she had caused him to feel sensations he hadn't allowed himself to even imagine in a long time. Emotions he thought had washed away on the tide that brought him to this island during a winter ocean storm. While he had told himself for years he couldn't afford exposure, since meeting this woman, he had questioned whether mere existing was living.

Standing beside a large pillar opposite the check-in reception, Toby rested his shoulder against the column and looped a thumb in the edge of his pocket. With a casual tilt of his head, he peered across the foyer.

Calvin addressed a guest, his features animated, hands flying around the air in illustration. The clerk's round face split with his easy smile, his eyes almost frog-like behind the rims of his trendy glasses, and Toby could see why Calvin was a beloved member of the staff at the Del.

Toby leaned farther around the edge but without spotting the object of his surveillance. No sign of the girl.

"You're not looking for me, are you?"

He jumped, and his forehead banged against the pillar. The voice from behind his shoulder startled him. Toby slipped away from the wall, and faltered two steps before regaining his balance. Losing his footing, he would have landed on the floor had he not grabbed the corner of the column. He regained his stance, embarrassment at being caught flamed before he was able to stand tall. Pulling at the hem, he adjusted his shirt back into place.

In her gold and sand-colored vest uniform with the beige skirt and matching low heels, she was even more striking than in her runners and baggy sweat clothes. She lifted a hand to hide her well-formed mouth, covering her snickers. Her eyes sparkled, the edges crinkled with mirth.

Heat and desire mixed a bold concoction to fire through his veins. At least a head taller, Toby looked down upon her, but the memory of her lips on his consumed him. Stomach clenched, he was lost as to his next move. Toby hadn't thought this through. He had been focused only on spotting her from a distance, gauging what she was like, then perhaps working up to actually talking. Now, faced with the need for more, wondering what it would be like to be with someone so bold—someone confident enough to know her own mind and be willing to chase it regardless of the fallout, he drifted in a sea of uncertainty. Struck dumb, Toby clenched his hands. How he craved such freedom. For so long he had lived a regimented, restricted life. Her kind of openness seemed as attainable as walking on the moon.

He unclenched his fingers from the column and scooped her free hand into his and pulled her through the corridors, past the back entrances to the many boutiques, to a secluded spot where they wouldn't be disturbed. This old building, as familiar to him as his houseboat, had been a second home since his arrival almost a decade ago. He didn't glance over his shoulder to check her reaction for he felt it in the way her fingers twined with his. The way he didn't need to pull her along, so much as lead the way. Her breath caught on a giggle while they raced down a narrow hallway, and her thumb drew light circles on the sensitive side of his wrist.

Reaching a small alcove, he pulled her into the cool shadows and turned her so her back braced against the wall. Her chest rose and fell in rapid breaths that matched his own. The pink flush on her cheeks was reminiscence of how she looked when she had been running, and his need grew. Keeping his fingers laced with hers, he braced his other palm against the wall by her ear.

She gazed up at him, her amber eyes flames waiting to be stoked.

He bent his head so his forehead touched hers, almost nose to nose. "I don't do this," he said with a voice he didn't recognize. He used a thumb and traced the line of her full lower lip.

Her tongue peeked between her lips before her front teeth followed to pull the bottom lip into her mouth. The sensuality of the movement made the molten desire she had ignited flame, and he breathed deeply to quell his rising need. Her eyes, so wide and full of mischief, gazed at him with a mixture of innocence and seduction.

"Do what?" A small dimple appeared to the right of her lips as she quirked a grin.

On a groan, he moved his hand to brace behind her neck, his thumb running along her jaw while lowered his head to hers. Their noses touched in an

Eskimo kiss, and he paused but a moment.

Then her teeth released her lips, and her mouth parted.

He tilted his head a fraction until his mouth could mold to hers. Electricity shot to the deepest part of his core, and he pulled her close. Her arm circled his neck, and she arched closer until her pelvis rubbed against his. She sighed and moved her lips along his jaw then bit the lobe of his ear. "Yes," she whispered. "You do *do this*."

A door slammed down the hall, and the sound, like an alarm, reminded him their private moment was fleeting. He pulled back and moved his hand to cup her cheek. "This isn't me. I don't *do this*."

"So you said," she replied with an impish grin, bringing back the memory of the pixie. Her gaze travelled from his eyes to his lips and back again. Then she ran her fingers through his hair. "I really wanted to do that."

He wasn't sure if she meant mess up his hair or kiss him. "Really?"

"Really."

At a loss for conversation after such a kiss, needing—wanting—more, he shrugged without a response.

She seemed to somehow understand and not be offended by his lack of words. Her smile widened, spread across her features, creating a glow, and she hooked her hands on either side of his face to pull his head closer. The kiss was chaste. "I have to get back to work. Break's over."

"Mine too."

Her eyelashes fluttered. "Quite a break for

someone who doesn't *do this*."

She was teasing. Toby chuckled. What could he say?

She started to move away.

He grabbed her arm with a light touch, enjoying the smoothness of her skin. "I don't know your name."

She shook her head and the dimple under her chin deepened before turning her gaze back on him.

The seductress was back and she again bit her lip, seeming to ponder her next words. After a prolonged pause, she finally spoke. "Why would you need to know?"

The air whooshed from his lungs. He realized he had been waiting for her answer. But she had sparked something in him, as well, and he found he liked the game. "In case I want to *do this* again."

She backed one step, yet her body swayed toward him. "But you don't *do this*." She made air quotes with her fingers on one hand.

He regained a hold on her hand. "I might change my mind," he replied, the words coming easily now. From where, he couldn't say. She drew a version of himself from the depths he had long ago buried. His thumb traced circles on the inside of her wrist, mimicking her earlier teasing.

Her gaze flickered down to his hand, and he noticed the pulse beat in her neck, the swell of her breast, the rise and fall of her chest. The thought of his effect on her quickened his emotions, sent a frisson of excitement along his veins.

"I hope you *do*," she said, her voice husky. She stepped away and trailed her fingers along the wall as she walked slowly out of their secluded alcove.

Glancing over her shoulder before taking the turn, she winked. "I hope you *do*."

Chapter Seven

The quiver behind her knees threatened to cripple her step. When she turned the corner, she stopped to brace a hand against the wall. A flutter flitted through her stomach. What just happened?

After a moment, Wendee continued with measured steps back through the corridors. The iconic resort, so large and sprawling, had additions she hadn't yet mapped in her internal GPS. Everything she passed, the landmarks, statues, the floor-to-ceiling portraits, were all seen through misty edges. Her mind felt filled with fluff, and she paid little attention to where her feet moved her. When would her heart resume a natural beat? Glancing up at the dark-paneled hallway, she prayed she wouldn't get lost as she returned to the lobby. She bit her lip to hide the grin.

The heavy concentration on her steps reminded her of when she was teenager returning home late after a party, having drank too much and trying to appear sober. Not that she could ever get much past Nan, despite her many attempts. Her own mother had put her grandmother *through the wringer*, as Nan was fond of saying, a wistful ring to her voice. Still, there wasn't much room left for Wendee to get away with mischief.

The memory cleared the fog. How she wished she could have known her mother. Yet, the pattern of relationships from her grandmother to her mother was what kept Wendee from engaging too much with boys in the first place. She shook her head. Then what was she doing?

Steadier now, she contemplated the family trend. Nan had told her about her being barely an adult when Alexis, Wendee's mother, had been born. Then Wendee, too, was a teenage product of her mother's involvement with an upcoming hockey star who bailed quickly after being told he was to be a dad. That he only returned after learning her mother was part of the Cavanaugh banking family did nothing to endear him to Nan's affections. When Alexis died from colon cancer, Wendee was too young to understand the circumstances of Nan paying off her father in order to retain custody.

"Best money I ever spent," Nan would say.

Having never accepted a handout, though, Wendee didn't learn until much later, Nan had given him nearly everything she had. In desperation to see her grandmother safely cared for, knowing Nan would never approve of her contacting her brother for money, Wendee went to work for Roger...

"Enough." Hands to her cheeks, she swiped her fingers across her eyes then fluffed her hair. At this moment, she was sure anyone who glanced her way would know exactly what she had been up to. To say she'd never done anything like that before was an understatement. Her avoidance of boys had led Nan, on several occasions, to broach the subject. But Wendee was adamant she wouldn't allow the same thing to happen to her that had happened to Nan and her mother. An occasional date when she felt compelled or the social engagement warranted, but high school, then college, saw brief flings with little sizzle. Then Nan got sick…

However, lately, with this guy—Toby—she seemed possessed by another being. What had come over her? What was it about him? Every time she saw the tall man with the chiseled jaw, she reacted like another person—more vivacious, flirty even. Even the stubble on his cheeks, so fair the whiskers made him appear golden and she couldn't resist. Like a magpie, she was attracted to the shine. Yes, she had hoped to see Toby again on her run, but she certainly didn't plan their encounter. She touched her shoulder and grimaced as she rounded the corner of the desk. Toby didn't fit in any of her plans.

"My, you look refreshed," Calvin commented when she took up her post. He paused filing check-in cards, his hair precisely messed. He reached a forefinger to lower his glasses just a bit over the bridge of his wide nose. His gaze raked her from head to toe, brows raised in question. "Where'd you go?"

To meet his gaze would give her away. So, after a quick glance, Wendee logged in and concentrated on the computer entries. She shrugged, noncommittal. "For a walk." From the periphery of her vision, she saw him replace his glasses.

"Judging by the glow on your cheeks, you look like you went for a run," he said with a chuckle.

Wendee chanced a hasty peek in his direction. "No, just hurried—"

"My turn," Calvin cut in, palm held up in the stop motion. "I'm off to see if I can catch those hunky SEALs on the beach exercising."

"I thought you had someone special?" Wendee asked, grateful for the change of topic. "Jared, isn't it?

You were telling me this morning you celebrated your one-month anniversary."

Calvin crossed the distance on his bandy legs, laid a hand on her shoulder, and leaned in close to her ear. He fluttered the fingers of his left hand. "No ring on this finger." He lifted his leg theatrically. "No chain on this ankle." Then he pointed to his eyes. "So, a fella's entitled to look."

Wendee giggled and waved him away. "Go on then, and keep an eye out for me too."

"Sure will," he called over his shoulder, already rounding the counter on his way through the foyer.

Barely a breath later, two guests approached, chatting. Hands animated, the younger of two ladies patted the shorter one on the back in a semi-embrace. "It's okay, Mum. I want to."

"But you don't have to," the mum said.

Turning her attention on Wendee, the younger laid her palm on the counter and smiled. "We're visiting from Canada…Mum's birthday trip—"

"My daughter," the mum interrupted. "She takes me away every year for my birthday."

"How nice." Wendee drew her hands together in front of her and steepled her fingers under her chin. She waited, used to guest hesitancy when they were about to request something they felt might be unusual, but not impossible, if you asked the right person.

"It's nothing, really." The daughter's cheeks flushed, and she draped her free arm over her mum's shoulders for a quick squeeze.

Witnessing the embrace made Wendee again wistful for a mother she never knew. What would life have been like if Nan hadn't given her father everything? Would they have taken trips like this to celebrate the greatness of Nan's life?

Wendee shook her head. Her grandmother would be angry if she knew Wendee showed any such regrets. Until that fateful night with the candle, they had made out just fine, thank you very much. Everybody, she reminded herself, had something to complain about—that wouldn't be her or Nan. Not then, and certainly not now. Keep moving forward.

Wendee smiled to encourage the mom and daughter. This kind of interaction with the clientele was one of the best things about working on the front desk of such a historic hotel. Meeting the great variety of people coming and going kept Wendee engaged and eager to come to work. Each day, with every conversation, she learned more about the world she so wanted to explore. Slowly, she was forming a bucket list of places she wanted to visit, if ever she were granted the opportunity.

Then the barrel of a pewter-colored gun filled her vision. She swallowed the lump of acid that rolled up from the pit of her stomach and clenched her fingers tighter. She wouldn't think of that. No. Roger lived in the past, and with each day, he became more distant. With a vigilant effort, he would stay there.

Instead, she focused on the positives of the moment. Wendee's supervisor, Susan, originally from England, told her the customers found Wendee charming, her curiosity endearing and caring. She strove to retain the good graces she'd forged.

The daughter looked down to the carpeting before returning her gaze to Wendee. "You see...I tried to reserve us into the restaurant for dinner tonight—our last night before flying home. I was told you're all booked."

"It's okay," her mum said. "Maybe she can recommend somewhere else."

The daughter patted her mum's hand but kept her focus on Wendee. Earnest hazel eyes compelled her assistance. "I know I should have reserved earlier, but really, we've been so busy taking in everything, and it's all my fault...I should have thought—"

Wendee held up her palm to halt the banter. "Just a sec, let me see what I can do."

"Really?" The mum looked hopeful.

Wendee fished the portable phone from the desk and held up a finger. Her smile widened with confidence. She knew just whom to call.

Wendee's cousin, Evangeline, answered the phone in two rings. "Hey, cos. Aren't you at work?"

"Yup, and I have a situation only you can fix."

"Good to know." Eva sounded intrigued.

In her mind's eye, Wendee envisioned the sandy-colored beauty scooting back from her desk, reaching to cross her ankles on the corner of her desk. Wendee laughed at the image.

Her cousin was an exclusive concierge consultant who specialized in extravagant, hard-to-obtain, one-of-a-kind events and packages for her ultra-wealthy clientele. Within a few moments, Wendee had brought Eva up to speed.

Eva placed her on hold for a moment and, within another five minutes the pair was reserved into what was considered the best restaurant in the San Diego area, complete with complimentary limo drop-off and pick-up. The ladies' faces glowed and the younger shook Wendee's hand. "This certainly means a lot," she gushed. "Unbelievable. How…I never expected there…how?"

"All in who you know," Wendee said with a giggle. "No problem, really. Actually, my cousin's a wiz at getting the exclusive deals. That's her job." Then she leaned closer to the desk, lowering her voice so not to be overheard. "You fly out tomorrow?"

"Yes, tomorrow in the afternoon."

A couple of minutes later, beaming with delight, the ladies left for their spa appointment with a small letter tucked in Mum's purse for safekeeping from Wendee, addressed to Nan's nursing home.

"Keep up the good work. We're all about service above self here," Susan said, her English accent musical as she stepped out from behind the small partition separating the front desk from the office.

Wendee gasped and cupped her hands together.

"Oops, sorry about that," her supervisor said, walking the length of the desk, checking each terminal with a sharp eye along her way. "What was that you gave the ladies?"

A frisson of guilt vibrated along her nerve endings. "Excuse me?" Oh, God, did Susan see the letter?

"The envelope?" Her British accent became clipped, her pinched nose flared.

Wendee faced Susan as the older woman walked, hand on hip, with stately grace toward Wendee. Skin the color of oranges left too long in the sun, Susan appeared to be a woman who thoroughly embraced the sun-kissed coast as opposed to what Wendee assumed was Susan's more rain-drenched upbringing in Britain. Tall, with cropped blonde hair and prominent green eyes, Susan conducted herself as though she was the owner and, according to Calvin, nothing got past her.

Wendee hoped this wasn't true. Certainly she had kept her interactions with the guests far from prying eyes.

"An envelope?" Wendee shrugged, searching for something, begging for inspiration. "I think it was in their mail slot. They had a blinking light on the room phone. I didn't pay much attention, just passed it over."

Susan's green-eyed stare didn't waver, but she blinked several times.

Amazed how easily the lie formed, Wendee resisted the urge to squirm under the intense scrutiny and held the older woman's gaze, her breath captured within her lungs.

At last, Susan clasped her hands and laced them to the waist of her skirt. "You're doing very well for someone with no prior experience. Keep up the good work."

Heart thudding against her ribcage, Wendee held her breath, which threatened to whoosh out with relief. She pinched her lips, turned to her keyboard, and waited for the clipped heels of Susan's departure before daring to release the pent-up air.

Then, without warning, Calvin skipped back around the corner from his break, straightening his khaki shirt over the beige walking shorts. He shook his head in regret, eyes creased with mirth. "No action outside today. Did I miss anything in here?"

"Just Susan pulling an inspection."

Calvin's dramatic features morphed, and he feigned a gag reflex. "The accent's fake, you know."

"No," Wendee said, unbelieving. "You're telling

tales again."

"True."

Calvin loved baiting her. Wendee might not be worldly, but she was fairly certain Susan didn't fake the accent. Too many of her mannerisms matched what she imagined to be European behavior. "You're the only one who says that." Wendee laughed. "You're trying to get me to start gossip."

"Am not—"

"Hey, Calvin." Toby lifted a hand before leaning a forearm on the counter. He turned and smiled in her direction.

So surprised by Toby's sudden presence, a squeak bubbled up her throat, and she coughed to cover her reaction.

Toby scratched behind his ear and smiled innocently before turning his attention back to Calvin. "Had a cancellation downstairs and thought I would stop by to check on the time of the next staff meeting. I lost the slip. Is it slated for this coming Monday? I knew you'd know, as chair of the employee committee, and wanted to make sure before I booked my dentist appointment."

Calvin fluttered his fingers and moved his computer monitor, hands flying across the keyboard. Then he pulled out a drawer just below the screen. "What would you guys ever do without us here at the front desk keeping track of everything?" He elongated the last word with a chuckle.

While Calvin had his head bent, Toby turned his attention to her. His gaze seemed to linger on her mouth, his own parting slightly, allowing his tongue to slip out to lick his top lip before capturing it between his teeth as though suppressing a grin.

A melting sensation filled her core, and she squirmed. Immediately, she was back in the secluded alcove with his lips upon hers, her hands twined in his hair. A deep pulse beat low in her abdomen, causing her heart to skip. She caught her breath and tried to look away, but he held her captive in his silvery gaze.

"Nope, not this Monday—next," Calvin said, breaking the tension. "Who do you see?"

"Umm, what?" Toby turned back to Calvin. His face had morphed from playful into confusion.

"Dentist," Calvin asked. "Who do you see?"

"Oh, just the guy in the clinic, down the way," Toby said, vaguely pointing a thumb over his shoulder. "So, a week from next Monday then?"

"Yes. Maybe you'll join us this time for drinks after?"

Wendee glanced between the two men. Clearly, Calvin wanted to keep the conversation going. There was a wistful note in her colleague's voice. She wasn't the only one smitten with the broad-shouldered masseur who fit her imaginings of the water god, Poseidon. Curly hair tied at his nape, skin the natural, golden color of healthy outdoor living, complete with trim muscles, both powerful and sleek, all held together, Toby embodied a hippy-casual look.

How could a guy who looked like Toby—six-foot massive, well-formed and perfect—not *do that*? Not kiss women? Not have ladies falling at his feet everywhere he went? It was all Wendee could do to not to wrap herself around him and beg for attention. She struggled to believe he didn't kiss women in out-of-the-way nooks within this historic property at every chance, but, according to Calvin, Toby was as pious as a monk. And somehow, the innocence reflected in his gray gaze made her believe him. His kiss had held the inexperience of a teenager with his first girlfriend, just discovering a natural attraction. Despite her reaction, his touch had been hesitant, making their encounter a delightful surprise.

He glanced at her again.

She didn't think she'd be able to hold it together much longer. Heat flamed her face, and within moments the ever-astute Calvin would guess their connection. The urge to touch him made her lace her fingers to hold them in place. She needed to distract herself from her wayward impulses. Wendee bit her lip—hard, concentrating on the pain to focus her thoughts. She needed this job. Whatever had come over her earlier had deserted her now. A dizzy sensation made her realize she was holding her breath again. What a day.

"Where are my manners?" Calvin said with a slap of his palm on the counter, shattering Wendee's trance. "Tobias, have you met the Del's latest addition? Miss Wendee Miller. That's Wendee, with a double E and no Y, that way you won't ask questions. Isn't that right, Wendee?"

Air whooshed out of her lungs, and she quickly inhaled. Wendee wanted to crawl under the ledge. Her vision turned white, and a lightness filled her with a fainting sensation. Her common icebreaker sounded absurd coming from Calvin. If only she could dive under the carpet. What could she say? She'd had no idea what motivated her mom to break with the traditional spelling of her name, but she had long since made a game of saying hers was a name where you never had to question "why."

Wendee squeezed her eyes closed and, when she opened them, realized one or the other of the men had spoken and expected an answer. She glanced between Calvin and Toby, opened and closed her mouth. Words failed. When nothing emerged, she folded her lips together and remained silent.

"That right?" Toby retreated marginally from the counter, his smile more fixed than genuine now. As he stared back, his brow tilted toward his eyes and several lines appeared on his forehead.

Searching his features, Wendee felt the façade of her earlier boldness melt away completely now that he knew her name. With the knowledge of her identity, there was no mystery left, and he would no longer be interested. She nodded farewell, at a loss for a conversation point.

He held his position a moment, his eyes large and questioning. "I thought I saw you out jogging the other morning?" he asked, slipping a hand in his pocket. "Along the boardwalk."

When Wendee didn't answer, Calvin jumped in. "That's right, I forgot you said you're one of those fitness addicts. Like you, Wendee, Tobias runs. I'll bet you did see one another out there."

Finally, Wendee found her voice. She shook her head. "I didn't say I was an addict. I think I mentioned I like to jog," she croaked.

Calvin flapped a hand. "Wears me out just thinking about it." He put a hand on his hip. "I forgot you like to run, as well, Tobias."

"Once in a while."

With Calvin's involvement in the chitchat, Toby retreated another step. The open playfulness of moments ago had closed down, and he angled his wrist toward his face, checking his watch. "I have to get back downstairs. The next guest will be there soon, if not already in the sanctuary. No one likes to be left waiting."

The playful cat-and-mouse game they had begun turned awkward. Again, Wendee had the impression of Toby's innocence—the cool mask, was simply that—a ruse that didn't come naturally to Toby.

Face full of mischief, Calvin leaned against the counter. "How come you're never available on staff days down at the spa? You have the reputation of being the best at what you do."

Toby's cheeks splotched with color. "I don't know about that." He began to walk away, seemed to remember something, and turned back to face them. "Nice to meet you, Wendee." His voice textured like honey liquefying in tea, for her ears only, dropping an octave. "Maybe I'll see you out running some time." With a swift turn, he strode across the foyer and disappeared around the pillar.

Wendee longed to follow and begin their game anew, but her courage had fled. This attraction to Toby had caught her unaware. Her reaction to him caused her to leave her guard at the door when she should be most careful with whom she associated. But she couldn't seem to help herself. These feelings were both foreign and natural at the same time. He brought out a playfulness she'd never experienced. Only when he was gone did she realize she had placed her fingers over her lips where his mouth had played only a short while ago.

Chapter Eight

In the name of self-preservation, Toby spent the next week hiding. He wasn't a coward. For sure, his mother didn't raise any cowards…but history proved otherwise…

Regardless, when he ran, he jogged early and changed up his regular route from what it had been when he met Wendee. When he worked, he stayed put, concentrating on clients' needs rather than his eagerness to satisfy his curiosity. Time to get back to keeping himself to himself. Whenever his feet led him through the corridors of the hotel to where he might "accidentally" run across *her*, he reminded himself how every day on this island was both borrowed time and a gift received from other people's sacrifice, and he returned to his rightful place.

Despite his efforts, Toby couldn't rid her from his mind. His stomach dropped to his feet with anxiety every time he imagined not seeing her. On days he decided not to lie, he admitted Wendee was more than a passing obsession. So many years alone had proven at least one thing: Toby wasn't prone to fancy.

Surrounded by the balm of the misty, aromatic air of the spa, Toby washed the oil from his hands, dried them on a fresh cloth, and walked the client back to the reception area.

Being away from Wendee and the glow she exuded

was like the start of a sugar fast, and he longed for the sweet taste of her lips on his, the way his hands so easily melded into her curves. Her vivacious personality played on his mind in an obsessive way. This preoccupation impacted his sleep, and the soft background music made him long for his bed and much-needed rest. That is, until he managed to retire alone and his imagination played havoc with his body, leaving him restless and unsatisfied with what was once his "norm." The last few nights had him waking in a sweat, pulse racing, and loins tight. Cold showers did little to relieve the tension.

He nodded to the receptionist and gathered a glass of flavored water for the client before she left. Instead of focusing on the next guest, he wondered where Wendee came from and what her story was. If there was one thing he had come to know about hotel staff, most were transplants from somewhere else and had a story to tell...or, like him, a story not to be revealed. He never probed.

Having completely forgotten when his next session was, Toby strode back through the hall and approached the staff area to pause just inside the door. Scarlett's schedule glowed on the touch-screen monitor to the right. He acknowledged the two other employees eating their lunch before he checked the timetable. He had planned on a full slate, but the next patron had rescheduled. "Damn," he muttered, scrolling down the electronic roster.

Joyce, the sturdy German practitioner, lifted her head from where she contemplated her sandwich and turned in his direction. "All okay there, Tobias?" Her accent was not as thick as it once was, but prominent nonetheless. In her eastern European way, Joyce insisted on referring to each of her co-workers by their given names.

"A cancellation," he muttered.

"No worries, we fill that spot." Her German accent left no room for connector words. She laid her lunch back in her lunch kit. With a palm flat on the table, she smiled and rose from her chair. "Staff day. We have a few overscheduled. More masseuse—that good. Check to see if they come early."

Toby held up his palms to stall her progress. "No, it's okay. I can fill the session." He made it a point to avoid conducting massages on fellow employees whenever possible. As a rule, he avoided staff days. How had he missed remembering this one? He shook his head and rubbed his temples—he knew. His distraction went by one name, Wendee Miller.

"Nonsense." She swatted his hands with a gentle touch. "I see you ready to work. So full of energy. I get you client."

From past experience, arguing with Joyce provided only a fruitless occupation. Resigned, he followed her into the spa courtyard, shoulders hunched in defeat. At this rate, he'd need a massage to relieve his tension. Offering therapy to hotel employees made him self-conscious. With guests, he presented a professional air never concerning himself about social interactions. The situation reversed for fellow staffers. Before, when he was new to the Del, he'd had experience with a couple of personnel who'd made more of the involvement—taking it from strictly professional to something of an assumed familiarity. From that point on, he avoided staff days like an illness. He gritted his teeth and kept pace behind his co-worker.

When she stopped, Toby pulled up short, narrowly missing bumping into her.

Joyce swung 'round to face him and leaned forward. "You like busy," she whispered, the "y" sounding like a "j" with her accent. "You, like me, hate the free time." She pointed to her chest. "This is just the ticket."

Toby shrugged, then straightened his shoulders and entered the room behind her. His gaze travelled over the people milling in the tropical garden, enjoying a fresh beverage or a bite to eat while they waited. Some read magazines while others simply dozed on the plush loungers. He searched for a familiar face, hopeful the employee wouldn't be someone he knew more than in passing—

Then his gaze locked on hers.

Wendee.

Toby froze to the spot, legs unwilling to carry him farther into the room. Conflicting responses of resisting the urge to turn and run warred with the desire to fold her into his arms and race to an empty room. Heart thudding, he forced himself to step up beside Joyce.

Wendee stood when her name was called and hobbled toward Joyce.

Color flared across her cheeks, and her wide eyes rounded. Her chest heaved with each breath. She flicked her gaze from his head to feet and back again before a small smile curved her lips. She returned her focus to Joyce. "Thank you," Wendee said, stopping in front of Joyce.

His stout colleague glanced between them, scrutinizing Toby with a furrowed brow. Joyce returned her attention to Wendee. "You know our Tobias?"

"We've been introduced." Wendee held out her hand. "You remember me, don't you, Tobias? From the front desk. You assisted me with a disgruntled guest a while back."

"We get a few of them here too." Joyce gave a nod of her head. "Our Tobias is good for soothing the situation."

Within a moment, her face had shifted from surprised shyness to coquettish seducer. Wendee's grin spread. "Yes, he's very good at soothing a situation."

"You look like you're in need of some therapy," Joyce continued, unaware of the double meaning.

"A pulled hamstring, I think," she said.

Then she turned to face him, and her tongue flicked out to lick her lips while her voice stroked him with a lover's caress. When her palm connected with his, a shiver laced his spine, and he felt his adam's apple bob, fighting to work. He held her hand, and his memory flashed to the alcove when her body had brushed against his.

"You okay there, Tobias?"

Joyce's stark voice recalled him to the fact he had yet to let go of Wendee's hand. As though stung, he released his grip, allowing his arm to drop to his side. "Excuse me. Yes, Calvin introduced us last week." The moisture on his upper lip tickled, and the muscles in his cheeks twitched in response. "Wendee's our latest addition to the front desk."

Joyce's chin jutted, and she nodded once. "Ya. Okay."

Wendee's eyes danced with mischief. "I tell our guests to always be kind to the front desk clerk. We can make or break their stay—upgrades and all."

Joyce crossed her arms in front of her ample bosom. "Ahh, yes, I see." Joyce started to turn. Then, as an afterthought, she added over her shoulder, "Be sure to remind them spa services will enhance their visit with us. We take away all those aches and pains. Make them friendlier to the front desk then, ya?"

"Yes, of course." Wendee smiled at Joyce before returning her attention to Toby.

Struck by the clarity of her tawny gaze, he forgot where he was and what was supposed to happen next until she reached to rub the back of her leg. Then she bent her head in the direction of her hand. "I should have no problem remembering that if you're able to get rid of this pain. I can hardly walk."

Toby covered his mouth and coughed. "Hamstring?"

"Yes." Wendee nodded. "I guess I've been running too much lately and not stretching properly before. You'd think I was looking for someone with all the miles I've clocked." She tilted her face toward Toby and smiled. "Susan suggested I come on down here and get fixed up before the injury turns into something more serious. She didn't like me limping all over the place. No need to draw undo attention, and all that."

"Yes, that sounds like Susan," he said in agreement.

Joyce had returned to the room with another of the practitioners. She stepped close and nudged him. "Our Tobias is just the therapist for you." Joyce patted him on the shoulder. "Our best."

"So I've heard," Wendee responded, her voice slightly husky.

Joyce nodded and strode away.

Toby stood for a moment too long, staring into the depths of Wendee's eyes. How had he not noticed the variety of color swimming together like the melting of caramel? Her lashes were longer than they first appeared. Blonde at the base, they darkened to a light brown at the end, leaving her with an open, unfettered look. Freckles danced across her nose and over her cheeks, both blending and enhancing her natural glow.

He shook his head to clear the thoughts and hide his mesmerized stare. "Shall we go?" He pointed down the hall toward the therapy rooms.

"Wherever you lead," she said, pulling the knot of the belt of her robe. "I will follow."

Toby's pulse quickened, and heat flooded to the unnecessary parts of his body. The next sixty minutes would test his professional capabilities. He closed his eyes and drew the eucalyptus-scented air deeply into his lungs. "Okay."

After showing her the room and pulling back the corner of the cover on the bed, he closed the door and stood out in the hall the customary two minutes to allow her to disrobe and crawl onto the heated massage table, facedown. He was grateful she lay on her chest so he could pretend she was just another client and not someone who occupied the majority of his thoughts. He knocked twice and cracked open the door a hair, just enough so his voice travelled. "Okay if I come in?"

"Of course."

Her voice carried back to him, sultry through the moistened atmosphere, heavy with scent. Or, was his imagination playing into reality? He stepped into the dim room and closed the door with a soft click before striding to the sink to wash his hands. "Are you okay with scented oil, or would you prefer unscented?" He forced his voice into a professional practicality, listing the choices. Then he inquired after the temperature of the table.

Her head was cradled in the nest of her arms. "The table is perfect. Nice and warm…not too hot, soothing." She lifted her face from the bed, propped her elbow, and rested her chin in her hand. "Comfy, really." Regarding him with a tilt to her head, she cooed, "Tell you what. You choose your favorite for the oil." And with that, she lowered her cheek to the table.

Toby dimmed the light then flexed and gripped his fingers before crossing the room to open the cupboard. He scanned the choices and made his selection from the array of vials. With a precise movement, careful not to drop the bottle, he hooked the canister to his belt so he wouldn't have to return to the workbench each time he needed more. He rolled his shoulders, pulled air in deeply through his nostrils, and, with a determination to stick to the task at hand, turned to face her.

Adjusting the blankets, he flattened his palms along her spine and applied pressure to each joint the entire length. Navigating around the table, he did the same for each of her legs and placed a pillow under her shins for comfort. He pulled her arm from the nest she created and, lifting the blanket, straightened it down to her side. He repeated the action on the other side, always applying pressure, getting a feel for tight spots while adjusting her body gently into a position more conducive to his practiced hands. Careful of her injury, he placed an extra pillow close to the tender area to avoid creating more pain.

"I thought you didn't massage staffers," she mumbled from the open face pillow.

With practiced precision, Toby folded the blanket until her back and arms were full exposed down to the swell of her bottom. "I don't." He retrieved a hot pack from the warmer. "I had a cancelation, and—"

"Lucky me."

His thoughts echoed the sentiment; however, he was fairly certain her quip of luck didn't match his vision. "Hamstring pull? You saw a doctor?"

"No. I didn't get to a doctor. I don't think it's necessary. More of a strain, really." She lifted her head and glanced over her shoulder. "I didn't stretch out properly the last couple of days and ran that vicious hill by the marina."

The marina? She couldn't know that's where he lived. Had she been looking for him, or was she teasing again? He couldn't tell. In all of his avoidance of her the last week, he could have easily bumped into her on his doorstep. "It's a tough climb if you're not used to the incline."

"When you're from the flats of Mis…"

When she didn't continue, he responded. "Sorry, I missed that last. The flats?"

Her head lifted then fell back into place. "It's my right leg."

Her shoulders had tensed. The cords of her neck tightened. Toby didn't press. He laid the warmed pack on her upper thigh, on the outside of the blanket so not to burn. The muscles rippled beneath his touch. Taking extra care, he arranged the pack where she suggested it hurt most and where, in his initial feel of her body, he detected the injury.

Her shoulders relaxed somewhat. He was rewarded with a deep sigh.

"Oh, that feels great."

Toby pumped the oil into his palm and worked the warm emollient through his fingers before taking his position beside the bed. "Let's hope you feel that way once I dig into the muscles."

Her shoulders rose and fell. "Here's hoping."

Did he have to read alternate meaning in everything she said? "I'll leave on the heat while I massage your back, neck, and arms, and return to the leg at the end. Any other aches?" His pulse had resumed somewhat normal pacing as he began the clinical assessment.

She giggled and the moment stretched. "Not really," she said, causing him to pause his motion. "But then again, *I don't do this*, so it's all new to me."

His words from her lips robbed him of composure. He made a show of returning to the bench to gather supplies he didn't need. Based on the inflection of her voice as she seemed to mull over some of the words, he had little doubt of her double meaning, taunting and teasing him. The vague "this" sent his thoughts into a whirl. Instead of commenting, he grinned, relieved she couldn't see the heat flooding his face, and returned to his post to begin the therapy. He pushed down lightly on her back in strategic places. Then he moved his hands to cup each side of her head. With her skull cradled in the cup of his hand, he lifted one arm and smoothed his palm down the length and maneuvered it to her side. He repeated the process with her other arm. Gently, he positioned her head so her face fit neatly in the cushioned hollow rest. "Close your eyes and relax.

Let the music and aroma wash over you. If at any time you feel pain or discomfort, tell me."

"Everything smells wonderful."

"We are a full body spa experience. Sight, smell, touch. When we're done, I want you rested, relaxed, and back in motion…without a limp." Toby smoothed his palms across her back again, applying pressure. He pushed deliberately along her shoulder blades, curving the cuffs of his hands toward her neck, checking her alignment. Then, with the same pressure, he moved down her spine. "How's my pleasure—up—oh—pressure?" He gritted his teeth and resisted the urge to bite his tongue.

"Perfect." She breathed the word.

He felt the suppressed giggle under his fingers. Damn. "I'm going down to fold the blanket farther, with your permission."

"Yes."

Her back was a pale peach, with tan lines crisscrossed. Here the freckles were patterned like the stars in the evening sky, beautiful to look at, enhancing rather than diminishing from her splendor. He pumped more oil onto his palms, rubbed his hands together, and then placed his hands along her upper back. Splaying his fingers wide, he spread the oil over her back, pausing a moment when she flinched as he ran his palm over a scarred abrasion on her right shoulder blade. "Oh, I'm sorry," he said, wishing the light was brighter so he could get a better look. While his fingers spread the length of her spine, he leaned closer. Under the dim lights, he made out the faded yellow bruising and the long, recently healed white scar, surrounded by raised red tender flesh that resembled a rash, almost burn-like, with healed welts. "I will avoid putting any oil or applying pressure along that area."

Her shoulder tensed. "I guess I didn't think of it when I came down. It's a…"

The back of her neck blotched, and Toby sensed her discomfort. As one who knew better than to pry, he traced his fingers up to either side of her head, rotating his thumbs along the back of her ears. "Looks like you bumped into something," he offered, giving her a way out. He downplayed how ugly and noticeable the wound appeared. Seemed unlikely by the looks of the injury that it had been seen by a doctor. Surely the width alone would have necessitated stitches. "You probably didn't even remember."

Her shoulders relaxed somewhat, and her neck muscles splayed loose under his working fingers. He moved his hands through her short hair, taking special note of the pressure spots at the base of the skull and to the side of the jaw.

That she had been injured knotted his gut. His hands hovered above her back, and he clenched his fists. With effort, he unclenched his fingers. He wanted to damage whoever had hurt Wendee. Familiar, but ancient, rage snaked along his veins. His heart ached with a possessive need to protect her. She may talk a good game, but the body didn't lie—tightly wound and hiding something, from someone. Had she run from an abusive partner? He craved to know her story, but how could he expect her to share when he was unwilling to do so himself?

After thirty minutes, he replaced the blanket over her back and moved down to address the reason for her visit—the hamstring. Within moments, he circled the knot with his thumbs and worked the edges to find the perfect placement for relief into the tight ligaments, feeling the release of the sinewy fibers. Concentrating small movements, Toby zoned, closing his eyes, envisioning the tissue, healthy, pink, and fibrous. He zeroed in on his target, pushing deeper with each pulse of his fingers. Movements precise and patient, he took his time, feeling the release of the tension.

Wendee groaned.

He remembered where he was. "Did I hurt you?" His hands didn't still, but he lightened his touch.

"No," she moaned. "Whatever you're doing, keep at it...feels wonderful."

What he wouldn't give to elicit such a response from this lady in other ways...

Chapter Nine

Well, it was official in Wendee's mind; he was more than a pretty face. Wendee lengthened her stride, tested the range of motion, and marveled at the ease of her gait when she took the stairs after the session with Toby. He had a magical touch, that was for certain. He seemed to pinpoint her aches and release them into nothingness. He even sounded different in the treatment room. A voice like liquid honey, it too, soothed to penetrate as deeply as his fingers.

She banged the cuff of her hand against her forehead. Stupid not to remember the bullet graze. She reached under her blouse to touch her shoulder blade, cringing at the rough texture of the skin. The wound didn't ache anymore, its placement just out of eyesight when she dressed in the morning. After all this time she had, amazingly enough, forgotten about it.

The ramifications of the near-miss staggered her. She shook her head and paused to grip the railing. Surely, Roger had no reason to search for her. She had nothing to do with the money going missing. The niggling little voice she tried to ignore reminded her of two facts. One, Roger believed she was indeed involved, and two, Roger never gave up.

"No," she exclaimed louder than intended. The sound bounced off the concrete walls. She looked around the empty stairwell to ensure she hadn't been overheard. All she would need is for people to start talking of her strange behavior. This island and her home with her cousin, Eva, was her fresh start. Evangeline had provided the opportunity, kindness, and more importantly, friendship. Wendee was not only grateful, but determined to make this new start work and, when the time was right, move Nan closer.

Nan would love the island. She had been so fond of telling her the story of Elleah and her brother Reginald, and how they met at this very hotel and then purchased the house Wendee now called home.

"Keep moving forward," she mumbled. Resuming her trek, she stretched her leg backward. Not even a twinge remained.

Focusing on the positive to think about the past sixty minutes, a smile sprang across her face. She rubbed a finger under her nose, and then pinched her lips gently between her finger and thumb. Stifling a giggle, she imagined what Toby's face must have looked like when she teased him. What was it about the brawny man that brought out the badness in her? She pictured the smock stretched across his broad chest. His upper arms swelling past the short sleeves, causing the fabric to bunch over his biceps.

No doubt, he was a hard nut to crack. Shy, or withdrawn? Or was this strictly a persona he adopted for work, because he didn't seem very reserved when he tugged her into the corner and kissed her? And the eye candy he presented the world didn't leave her in much doubt the effect he would have on the female staffers, never mind the variety of women he'd treat on a daily basis.

Come on, handsome, don't tell me you don't "do

that."

She dropped her hand to her neck and traced her fingers along her collarbone. The minute slick of oil softened her skin, and friction from her circling fingers re-released the essence. Did he massage everyone the way he touched her? She would have to assume so. That was his job, wasn't it? But, to be so intimate. Her insides quickened.

Heat flooded across her body, tingling everywhere his hands had been. Slightly intoxicated from the experience, she floated across the lobby, taking little notice of the ornate furnishings and stylistic flowers that normally captured her interest. The crowds buzzed around her like a honeycomb. Sunlight blazed in wide shafts across the antique tiles.

Despite her best efforts to goad Toby, he remained clinical and, after a while, she'd simply settled into the comfortable luxury of the massage. Only now, dressed and removed, did she allow herself to wonder what making love to Toby would be like. How she could imagine tracing her fingers across his firm abdomen, along his muscled thigh, seeking a response in kind. Her thighs tightened, and her breath quickened. Perhaps he could teach her some of the basics and allow her to massage him. With a racing pulse, her heart jackhammering in her ears, she envisioned gripping his broad shoulders, wrapping her legs around—

"That good, was it?"

Calvin's voice cut through her fantasy, and Wendee tripped over a speck in the floor, recovering her balance by reaching out both hands to the desktop. She hadn't realized she had made it across the foyer, back to reception, and taken up her position by rote, rather than by thought. She blinked several times to regain her focus. Then she shrugged and picked up a stack of entries. Unable to contain the giggle, she glanced to Calvin, who waggled his eyebrows.

"Word is you got our mister Tobias. How'd you manage that?"

Hotel gossip spread lightning fast. Wendee decided to avoid the denial and winked at her co-worker. "Luck of the draw, I guess."

"I'd say." Calvin traced his gaze from her head to her feet. "You're walking better."

How the comment made the mind wander farther into the depth of her recent thoughts, beyond what would be considered decent for a co-worker. With effort, she struggled to focus. "You'd never think I even strained the hamstring," she said and walked in a small circle, ending with a pirouette. "Gone. Like it was not ever there."

"A miracle," he announced in faked Holy Roller voice.

She and Calvin worked well together. They had a natural symmetry, complementing each other's work behavior, and were often paired on their shifts. She didn't mind a bit. Effervescent and dramatic, Calvin made the hours fly. She enjoyed his company more every time they shared a desk. More banter followed, with the remainder of the evening passing in a blur of activity. Calvin kept the tension low and the energy high, never sweating the small stuff, addressing the larger issues from diva-like guests with an expert hand.

There were eight front desk staff in total that alternated their times over three shifts—morning, afternoon, and overnight. She'd shared shifts with two other desk clerks. None were as exuberant as Calvin. She'd barely chatted with the two overnight clerks. They tended to mumble and exude an air of general grumpiness. She couldn't blame them, really.

"They're monsters," Calvin had said of the night auditors, eyes wide, almost innocent while he lifted a hand dramatically to cover his mouth while he whispered. Behind their counter, they watched the small woman with the steel-gray hair march through the lobby as though getting ready for roll call, instead of preparing for her shift. "The number crunchers are the worst. No fun at all."

"In a place like this, you'd think they'd be partying all the time," she returned, watching the older woman go through her checklist. "Get the slips from the merchants, log them into the accounting system, out of the way right away, and then enjoy the rest of the shift without incident. It's not like they have to deal with the volume of people we do."

Carol, a broad-built woman with small, piercing eyes glowering behind steel frames, grunted a hello. She muttered to herself something about having to spend the first hour each night fixing the mess left by the day staff.

As Calvin had conveniently vacated the premises, and no one else seemed to pay any attention to the complaints, Wendee sidestepped to her post, and ignored them as well. Once she was sure Carol was logged in and ready, Wendee logged off, checking the time to when she could officially punch out. She shrugged out of her uniform jacket and slung it over her shoulder, ready to go.

Calvin appeared in front of the counter. He tossed

his head to the side, reminding Wendee to make her escape. Within moments, she joined him.

He smiled and fanned his fingers to Carol, who lifted her gaze briefly from the screen. The intensity of her sharp look cut across the distance. Without a backward glance, Calvin took Wendee by the arm to escort her across the foyer to the staff area. "See, definitely monsters."

Wendee retrieved her bag, a carryall, from her locker in the ladies' area. She was just draping it over her shoulder when she noticed Carol standing in the doorway. Wendee glanced around the room, but she knew she was alone. Calvin had run off to the bathroom. "Y-yes?" she stuttered, a sudden nervousness of having been caught out for making fun clenched in her stomach. She cleared her throat and started again. "Did I forget something? Did you need something before I leave?"

The woman's small eyes, highlighted by the goggle-like frames that consumed her face like a frog, bobbed a bit, before she pushed them up the bridge of her nose with the knuckle of her middle finger. "Did you get the message?" Her lips stretched across her face, seemingly from ear to ear, without any hint of teeth, reinforcing the amphibious image.

"Message?" Who would leave her a message? Toby? Wendee's heart kicked up a notch. No. Carol only worked the overnight shifts, so the message would be from the previous night. Toby didn't say anything when she saw him. Would he say anything if she didn't? Damn, she couldn't read him.

The woman took hold of the arm of her frames where they met over the ear and adjusted them again.

"Very perplexing, really. This is your place of employment, and we're not supposed to receive personal calls." She shook her head.

"Yes, I understand, Carol." Pulse pounding, Wendee adjusted her bag over her shoulder for want of something to do with her hands, wondering how she could make a getaway without appearing rude. Should she remind Carol the desk sat unstaffed at the moment? She gripped the handle of her holdall, breathed deeply through her nose, and waited. "Perhaps whoever called didn't have my number." She didn't know what to say to prompt Carol to release the information and put her out of her anxiety. Carol didn't need to know Wendee changed the cell phone SIM card, her number, everything when she left Minneapolis.

When she left…certainly not—

Carol's tight curls reminded Wendee of steel wool.

Without volunteering further information, Carol flipped through the shift receipts. "Doesn't matter," she said, continuing perusal of the papers. "Didn't leave a name. Thought you'd probably know who it was and said as much on the note. I also said no more personal calls on my shift."

The snake Wendee had finally started to bury, becoming comfortable in her new life, uncoiled in her gut. "I didn't get the note."

"Damned twit from the morning shift," Carol said and started to return in the direction of the desk. "Knew she wasn't bright enough to pass along a simple message. All she does is complain about having to work so early. Should be glad of the job, I say."

Nausea washed over Wendee, and she felt the room tilt. Was it a man or a woman who called? Surely it wasn't the nursing home. She had Eva check on her grandmother regularly. She rushed after Carol, catching her after a couple of steps, and touched the older woman's shoulder, then backed away. "Please, Carol, can you tell me what the message was? A man or a woman?" The serpent began to rattle its tail, and a fog hugged the corners of her vision.

"Didn't know he was calling California, I'll tell you that." Carol didn't halt her stride to the guest counter. Resuming her perch, she picked up her calculator and began to arrange sheaves of printouts from the various facilities within the hotel: the bar, restaurant, shops, and spa. "Bloody strange. Asked for you, but wouldn't give a name. Said he was an old friend, and you would know who he was."

Wendee laced her fingers together over the grip of the handle of her backpack. "That's it?" Her breath stilled, and spots danced in front of her vision. *No*, the word screamed in her head.

"Yup. Said just to let you know your old friend called to catch up." Carol narrowed her sights and shot her a gimlet stare over her shoulder. "No personal calls."

Wendee lowered one of her hands to grip the counter and find her balance. She forced a smile and nodded. "I understand. You didn't happen to tell him where we are?"

Carol turned, almost a full circle on the spot. The glasses slithered down the shine of her nose and she pushed them back with her pinkie. "He called here. We all answer the phone the same, announcing the hotel by name. Wouldn't he know where he was calling?"

Wendee bowed forward slightly and backed away

from the front counter. "I imagine so."

Roger.

Time's up.

****

Everything good she had concentrated on prior to that moment zeroed into an all-engulfing black hole. With a dejected shuffling of her feet, Wendee exited the hotel. Calvin offered to give her a lift to her place, but going home and making small talk with Eva, pretending everything was normal, didn't offer any comfort. She tried to regain some of the jovial air from their shift then shrugged. "The strain on my leg made me miss my run today. I think I'll walk."

Her friend tilted his head and looked at her quizzically. Without a doubt, he'd noticed the change.

"You sure?" He brushed a hand along her sleeve. "I won't bite."

She laid her hand over his and shook her head. "Oh, if only you would," she countered, drawing a guffaw and flapping of fingers like wings.

Calvin pulled her into a hug. "Wendee of the doodle dees," he chided. "If only you were my type, we'd be perfect for one another."

"Go on." She pushed at his chest. "You say that to all the girls."

He strode away to his car, blew her a kiss, and waved. "Be safe, my dear pet."

"On an island polluted with Navy SEALs and Marines? I think I'll be fine."

He skipped off across the parking lot.

Wendee followed the sidewalk around the historic building. At the fountain, she stopped and peered down Orange Avenue where it connected with Ocean

Boulevard. The streets were basically empty on a sleepy Wednesday evening, save for the odd car and the bus idling at the stop in front of the coffee shop. Even the seabirds scarcely cried at the late hour.

She had been stupid. Wendee had become too comfortable in her new life. Of course, she had never intended to live a life on the run. She was a bookkeeper, for Christ's sake. Wendee leaned over and gripped her middle, wrapping her hands about her hips. Rushing to the side of the pavement, she clung to a trashcan and emptied the feeble contents of her stomach.

He'd found her. Roger. Wasn't it enough he almost killed her once? Her need for cash to support Nan when she'd become invalided had made her work for a known criminal, all the while thinking if she carried on and just did her job, she'd be fine. The criminal element wouldn't impact her.

Then she had naively assumed, after all this time, he would have realized she could never have stolen the $2.4-million he accused her of skimming over the two years she worked for him. When she agreed to the position at the bowling alley, she'd had no idea of the main source of revenue. Hadn't he realized she drove the same beat-up car, lived in the same single-bedroom apartment, didn't indulge in fancy trips, or wear expensive clothing? All her money went to the nursing home to pay for the comforts so deserved by her grandmother. Just where was she spending all the extra loot? Roger had accused her of giving the money to the Steeple brothers. So, to his mind, she not only stole the funds but played Robin Hood and gave it away as well. My God, she hadn't even heard of those bastards until they started to follow her, showing up at Nan's residence home and bumping into her when she picked up groceries.

Then there was the scene at the coffee shop within the bookstore when Roger walked in and caught her just as she had finally worked up the courage to confront the two hoodlums and find out what they wanted.

"What am I going to do?" she muttered and turned to follow the path between the cottages back toward the beach. She staggered. Her head swam. What would Roger do? His plan would be a simple elimination if a knowledge of his past predicted the future. Did that mean he was on his way now? Surely he couldn't know where she lived. If he did, how would she tell Eva?

She drew a breath and calmed her racing pulse, praying the snake would return to its coil. She held her head between her hands. She told herself she had no need to panic—yet. Obviously, Roger wasn't here. But that didn't alter the fact he had found her. Now it was only a matter of time.

She stepped off the boardwalk, and her feet sank into the sand. The tiki torches provided arches of light across the beach. She glanced one way then the other. The expanse of coast seemed empty, the ocean invisible in its blackness. Even the Del, to her back, lay at peace, the groundkeepers having finished and the next shift not due to start until four in the morning. The evening damp chilled her, and she shivered.

Her letters to Nan. Damn. Had her grandmother even received one? How had Roger gotten one or all? Was Nan safe? My God, spots swirled. How could she involve Eva further without placing her in danger? No, she couldn't do it. There would have to be another way.

Would Roger come all on his own or send henchmen? For revenge, sure, he'd come himself to make sure the deed was completed. Could he really still think she had the money? Or suspect she had approached the authorities? Now she wished she had. She dragged her fingers through her hair and pressed the heels of her hands to her temples.

She had thought she was so smart, leave her troubles behind. Keep moving forward, as Nan had always said. Yet, she had retained the ledgers. Even now, they lay tucked under the bed like an insurance policy. Some insurance. She had endangered everyone she loved.

Her bag slid down her arm and hung off her elbow. Her blood ran hot and cold, all at the same time. She dropped her arm, letting the knapsack slip into her hand. With a burst of rage, Wendee spun in a circle and threw the sack, contents and all, across the beach. She covered her face with her palms and moaned, dropping to her knees. Cradling her cheeks in her cupped hands, she leaned forward so her elbows connected with the ground. She couldn't change the past, and now she was alone without options.

Sand slipped into her shoes, and she sat back on her bottom, kicked off the sandals, and chucked them after her purse. She fisted handfuls of sand and threw clumps until her arm hurt. Raising her knees, she leaned forward until her arms were supported by her legs and let her head droop. Tears threatened, but didn't fall.

After a bit, her breathing slowed and her mind cleared. She had time, she repeated over and over again. She repeated the mantra from before. She needed time—more time to plan. There had to be time. Time to do things right. Disappear where no one would know her. How long until he'd get here, she didn't know, but Roger wasn't here today, and with that reprieve, she would devise a strategy.

Think. Stop, be still, and think. Then plan. She banged her fist against her knee. She would see Nan safe and plan her escape.

"Bad day at the office?"

Wendee jumped, her hands gripped across her heart. A flashlight illuminated her position, and Wendee shot to her feet, stumbled, and fell back to the sand. She scrambled for purchase, blood pounding in her ears, while the breath whooshed out of her body. "What? Who?"

Chapter Ten

Toby fumbled the small penlight while he tried to flick it off. In his haste, he missed and dropped the flashlight to the sand. Bending, never taking his gaze from Wendee's shrunken form, he stashed the cylinder in his back pocket. He groaned inwardly. Realistically, he should never have followed her to the beach. Resuming his height, he held out a palm. "It's okay." He took a half step toward her, one hand extended.

She rounded up on her knees, getting one foot firmly positioned in the sand.

She reminded him of a sprinter on the blocks, ready to bolt. When the silence stretched, Toby tried again. "It's only me. I'm sorry I scared you."

Wendee rolled up, both feet under her, hands braced on her thighs. Shoulders hunched, her head folded down to her chest. Then she hissed under her breath, "What the hell..."

"I know..." He let the words hang as he dropped to sit on the damp sand. He left a good distance in between. She could leave or stay, he would leave the door open. "Bad timing," he said after another minute. Seemed the story of his life, *sometimes.*

In the dim light from the beach lanterns, he watched her take her head in her hands, fingers splayed through her short hair. "No shit." Still bowed in prayer position, she lowered her arms to wrap them across her chest and grab her shoulders. She tilted her face toward him. "You stalking me?"

He ran fingers through his own hair, sighed, and laid his hands onto his lap. If she only knew how close he came to violating the ethics of his profession this afternoon. Stalking her would be the least of his concerns, if he had his way. Today, he had been permitted to *touch*, but not allowed to *feel*, and how he wanted to feel.

To have her lithe body beneath him. Feel her warm breath on him. Taste her lips. Listen to her sighs and know he had drawn the emotion from her. The power of connection. The simplicity of joining. The lasting consequences.

No, stalking was an understatement to the depth of his intention when her fifty-five-minute massage session had come to an end. Shaking his head, he wracked his brain for a reasonable denial to her question, gave up, and twisted in the sand to view her squarely. Seeking a diversion, something to change the conversation, and perhaps bring back her usual vivacious spark, he grasped at the first item to come to mind. "I'm curious about the letters."

Like a gopher in a prairie field, she straightened— alert. She hung her arms to her sides, and her shoulders firmed, while her chin kicked up a notch.

Even in the semi-darkness, her eyes seemed to glow with an intensity, peering through him instead of at him. "What are you talking about?" Her voice croaked.

Could he say nothing right tonight? He began to sweat and rubbed his palms together. He wanted to escape the awkwardness of the moment. Where had the easy comfort and the fluid flirting gone? Had their time together at the spa ruined everything when he had hoped it would be a beginning? How foolish he was to dare to hope. He should have known better. That type of fantasy didn't include him.

Toby stared through gloom, opening and closing his mouth, seeking articulation. Nothing. He licked his lips and sighed. How he ached to find some remnant of the spark that had, until this afternoon, so easily arced between them. Her eyes were wide in a face gone pale and reflected back the limited light. Even in the shadows, she appeared drawn.

Toby resisted the urge to flee. Instead, he sat forward so his elbows rested on his raised knees, and he let his fingers dangle. Looking out to sea, the clouds scuttled across the horizon. Releasing his breath, he scooped a handful of sand to let it sift through his fingers. "I'm not sure really." He smiled, giving up any notion of salvaging the evening. "Just looking for conversation because I enjoy your company. I've seen you hand letters to departing guests and, because I haven't seen any of the other staffers do this, I was curious."

He thought he'd picked a topic of little consequence. Something a little less volatile than his attraction and subsequent stalking. The stiffness of her posture told him he was on a roll of picking all the wrong subjects. But now he had asked and, devil be damned, he stuck to it. He'd leave if she asked him to, but for now, he had nowhere better to be. Being with Wendee saying all the wrong things was still better than being alone on his houseboat. He linked his fingers and rolled his thumbs over one another, at a loss for what to say next. When all else fails, shut up, is what his Da used to say.

"You," she said, and paused as a seabird cried in the distance. "You like my company?"

Surprised, he glanced over at her. "Yes."

"Ha," she said. With a sudden motion, she bent and retrieved her bag and shoes then stalked off, sand flying in her wake.

She would have clipped his arm had Toby not skidded out of the way. By the time he gained his feet, she was halfway to the boardwalk. He caught up to her within a couple of strides.

She glanced at him. "I have to go," she said, making her way toward Ocean Boulevard, tossing the backpack over her shoulder.

"What the hell…" he muttered, wondering whether he should stay with her or let her go. A rollercoaster had begun in his stomach, and he felt nauseous with the indecision. He couldn't leave her. Not in this state. Whatever happened was serious, and no one should be alone like that.

"It's late," he said. "Let me walk you home." Sure, the island boasted one of the lowest crime rates in the country, but they weren't immune, and it was after midnight. "I've upset you…I mean…I didn't mean—"

"It's not you," she shot over her shoulder. Her steps slowed, and she twisted to pace backward, her steps awkward and appearing as though she would tumble over at any moment. "It is…ahhh…but not now." She bit her lip, then shook her head and resumed walking facing forward again. "It's not you," she repeated with a firmer tone. "I just…I have to go."

He knew she lived with her cousin and she'd be

fine once she got home. Toby thought of girls like pack animals; once they were in the comfort of each other's company, all would be well. But to see her so upset, and by herself, he couldn't let her go on alone. Unlike their previous encounters where her personality filled a room as a giant, at the moment, she seemed so vulnerable and small. He ached to take her in his arms and soothe her anxieties. Like him, he sensed something weighed her down. He hesitated to ask, even though he doubted whatever she had to hide barely scraped the surface of the noose that typically dangled invisibly from his neck.

Still, she kept walking while Toby delayed, wrestling with his thoughts. She bounced up on to the boardwalk, and then quickened her pace. The tread of her bare feet echoed off the wooden planks. "I'm fine," she repeated.

She seemed to be speaking more to herself than him. He reached for her arm, but dropped his hand before making contact. "Listen, I'm sorry," he said, matching his tread to hers. He held up his palms. "Really, I seem to be doing and saying all the wrong things tonight, and all I wanted to do was talk."

Wendee shot him a glare, brows raised. "Really? You wanted to talk? Because you *like my company*."

The words sneered, ugly and cheap. He winced and she chuckled, but it was a sound without mirth.

"You follow me down to the beach to talk? Even though you *don't do that*," she said, making air quotes with one set of her fingers. "Is that your shtick? Use your crooner's voice. Come on all innocent and shy, make the girls do all the work, while telling them *you don't do that*."

How had he hurt her? It certainly hadn't been intentional. But by the tone she used, Toby felt as though he had led her on. Had he? He'd been so selfishly concerned about his own needs, his own wants, what he does and doesn't do, had he inadvertently stepped on her heart to cause her voice to reveal such pain? "No." Toby braced his fingers against his temples to figure out where everything went sideways. "I really don...haven't...I never—"

Wendee stopped. She re-slung her bag over her shoulder, where it had slipped down to the crook of her arm. "What?" she demanded, hands braced on her hips. "I let you know I'm interested. You play coy and avoid me. We kiss, then you hide... You have h-hands like a magic conductor making my body feel...oh...forget that... Now, you're here...but then he called. For God's sake, make up your damned mind—"

Toby reached for her shoulders, catching the tremor in her voice, and a well-tied knot settled in his gut. "Who called?"

Her eyes, like liquid, large and round, glared up at him. Fear colored the honeyed depths.

"What? Who?" Her voice had risen to a hoarse whisper.

"You said, 'then he called.' Who called? Are you in trouble? Let me help." Toby knew he shouldn't ask. He shouldn't offer. But hadn't he been self-consumed for long enough? Her business was her business, sure. Realistically, if he couldn't share with her, he had no right to ask her to confide in him. Yet, here he was, and that was exactly what he intended.

She shook her head and tried to jerk away. "It's not you."

"Maybe I can help."

Wendee tugged out of his hold. Bending, she slipped the sandals back on her feet then straightened and seemed to firm her spine. A tear glistened in the soft light. "No one can help me."

On impulse, he pulled her against him. She braced her palms on his chest as though contemplating resistance, but she didn't push him away. Her hands warmed his skin through the thin T-shirt where he hadn't realized he had gone cold. Like he could see the pulse beat in her neck and the heave of her chest, he knew she could feel the pounding of his heart, but he didn't care. He folded a finger under her chin.

She lifted her gaze to him.

As he stared down into her rounded eyes, he tried to read her. His thumb stroked her collarbone, and he lowered his mouth to hers. With a sigh, her lips parted, and her tongue flicked out to touch his.

A sizzle started low in his loins, and fire scorched his veins. His arms slid around her slender waist to hold her close. Tracing the curve of her spine, he lowered his palms to the small of her back, a hair's breadth from the swell of her bum.

Wendee twined her hands around his neck and wound her fingers in his hair. She arched a fraction away and touched her nose to his. "Tell me what you want?"

Electric currents fired along his nerve endings, and only they existed in the world. Curiosity fled as their chemistry ignited. "You," he said simply, breath ragged. "But, I don—"

She stiffened in his arms and would have yanked out of his hold had he not held her firm. "Not this again." She lowered her head so her brow connected with his jaw.

Toby breathed deeply of the scent of her hair. Would this be the last time he ever stood this close to her? Time to cut bait or go home, as the fishermen from his small town would say. He had to trust someone, some time. The memory of his town brought his mother to mind. Her courage. The ability to stand tall despite the storm. She always said he had good instincts about people. At this moment, he was willing to throw all his chips in the game and gamble on Wendee Miller. Perhaps, if he trusted her, she would trust him, and together they could find a way. "Let me finish." He tightened his hold.

She sighed but nodded. She lowered her hands to rest along his upper arms.

He took a large gulp of air. "Before you...I've never kissed a woman."

She snapped back her head, and her gaze searched his face. "Wait...what?"

Heat flushed his skin. Glad of the cloak of darkness, he pulled in air through his nose, preparing to continue. "You're the first—for me. First woman I ever kissed."

Her hands fell from his biceps and released his grip. She stepped back. Toby returned her stare and waited.

She lengthened the distance between them. Her fingers flicked in front of her, illustrating his body from head to toe. "How..." She stopped then chuckled, and seemed to wait for his response as though there were a punchline. When he didn't respond, her face straightened. "How is this possible? You—

you're…so…"

Toby opened his mouth to answer, but the words lodged in his throat. He shrugged. A trickle of sweat dripped down his spine.

She wobbled her head from side to side and bit her lip. Her hands lodged on her hips. "You're not ga—"

His hands shot into the air, palms faced out, halting her words. "No, nothing like that."

"S'okay if you are," she returned, mouth puckered. Mirth creased her eyes. "I just don't want to be somebody's experiment."

Toby reached for her hands and traced his thumb across her wrists. "No…I just…I was…never been…no opportunity," he ended feebly. He groaned. No, that wasn't true. There'd been plenty of opportunity. There was no easy way to explain the situation. He lowered his head. "Fuck!" he groaned, then glanced up quickly. "Sorry."

Wendee giggled, the familiar dimple pinching her cheek. She stepped closer. "Take your time."

Toby shrugged. "Maybe we can walk a bit."

She glanced around. "Where?"

Toby inclined his head south. "We could walk to the marina." He took her hand.

They changed directions and started off down the sidewalk in front of the hotel. When the time stretched, leaving so much unsaid in the air between them, he glanced over at her. "What's wrong? Do you want to tell me?"

She dropped his hand, but continued to match his stride. She shook her head. "No…ah…nothing's wrong… Never mind."

Then she seemed to change her mind and stepped

back to his side.

She inclined her head, lifting her chin. "This is my direction, anyway." She smiled and re-laced her fingers with his. "The island's pretty small. Basically, anywhere wouldn't be far from where anyone lives."

Toby knew where she lived. He had followed her more than once, never knowing how to approach her without scaring her. When Wendee detoured to the beach this evening, he saw his chance. But something was off. She was hot and cold at any given moment. Like a hare scared by the light, he felt she could bolt at any second.

Wendee leaned so her shoulder brushed against his arm. "Not now, okay? I need some time to figure out things."

Toby brushed his lips along the crown of her head. He respected her response. Her fingers squeezed his as she fell in step beside him.

The movement eased the snakes in his gut, creating a sense of comfort. Being with her in any capacity seemed so easy, he wondered if he had known her all of his life, even before they met. They strolled in silence and, for the first time that evening, there was no strain. They left the hotel property behind and continued under the canopy of trees. The fragrant flowering bushes surrounded them with their aroma.

Content, he said, "This is nice." He felt her nod, her head brushing against his biceps.

Then, after a while, she glanced over at him, eyes squinted and brows wrinkled over her nose. "I'm sorry." She lifted her fingers to brush her bangs from her brow. "But I simply can't fathom it." Wendee moved her fingers to play with the small dangling earring in her left ear. "I don't mean to sound like I'm bragging here, but I've kissed my fair share of men and...not to swell your head or anything...you do the deed like a pro."

Toby coughed, rubbed a knuckle under his nose, and proceeded to scratch his head. "Thank you," he managed, the heat returning to creep across his face. "I guess." He shrugged, at a loss as to how else to comment.

Wendee squeezed his hand and, when he looked down, she grinned.

Mischief glinted again. Her usual spark returned, giving her the look of an impish fairy in the moonlight, surrounded as she was by the foliage along the walkway. "It's not that I didn't want to..." He coughed again and lowered his hand to tuck his thumb into his pocket. "Can we just leave it that I have lived a fairly solitary life and chose *not* to involve myself with anyone?"

Wendee laughed. "Why, are you on the run from the law or something—"

He tripped, and his head snapped to attention. "Why would you ask that?" He halted his step and dropped her hand.

"I was just joking..." She stopped too, to scrutinize his face. "Toby?"

Her face had lost its mirth, and a pucker framed her eyes.

A dog growled in the yard behind them.

"It's okay to tell me." She linked her hands in front of her and rhythmically swayed up on her toes, then back to her heels, repeating the motion while she waited for a response.

The dog scratched against the fence, his low tone menacing.

Toby peered over her shoulder, pressing a hand to her back to encourage her to move along the sidewalk. He glanced at her. "I don't know if I can."

"Then no it is." Wendee scooped his hand back into hers, turned, and continued walking down the road. Toby followed her lead.

"You are a gentle man, Toby. I know this—I *feel* this," she said, casting him a look. "And...unfortunately, I *know* the difference."

He wanted her to tell her secret. Who had hurt her? He raged against whatever had caused her pain. The war of exposure struggled in his gut, curling the snakes of indecision. They crossed over the bridge and rounded the harbor entrance. The night was silent, the darkness offering the peace of a confessional. As though by mutual consent, they stopped to sit on a bench under an orange tree.

He drew a deep breath and laid his free hand over the top of their laced hands. He contemplated the power of his hand. Its ability to cause so much pain. Its ability to heal through strategic touch. He settled their linked fingers on top of his leg, the connection with another person necessary to get through the story. He gulped. It was time to end the battle. "My sister died when I was eighteen."

"I'm so sorry," she said quietly and gazed up at him, her eyes filled with sympathy.

He lightly squeezed her fingers. "Really, she was a pain in my ass most of the time. A real know-it-all." He laughed, and the sound stuck in the lump in his throat. "Carrie was the best person I knew, and I loved her."

The time had come. On the breeze, he felt the whisper of his sister releasing him from his guilt. "We were very close. Less than a year apart in age. But, because of me…" He lifted his hands from her hold and held them out in front of him to contemplate. Then he dropped them to his lap. "She died."

Chapter Eleven

Wendee sat on the wooden bench. The seat retained some warmth from the day. Toby lowered his bulk with the grace of a statue, stiff and unyielding. She settled close, but too close. Their thighs aligned on the bench, but she held herself as still as she could. She didn't want to distract Toby from the confessional. His pain was visible on his earnest features. His lips had thinned into a tight line, and his jaw muscle clenched.

Wendee burned with a desire to help him settle his soul, certain he had not—as he indicated—aided in the death of his sister. Perhaps an accident caused this guilt. She could imagine a sibling's conscience if they were present at the passing of a loved one. Surely, whatever caused him to live the life of the monk was not comparable to her having a known associate of a crime family after her, thinking she stole millions of their ill-gotten dollars. She drew a shuddered breath, held it, and released the air slowly. In and out—hold—in and out...she wouldn't think of Roger just now. Fingers linked in her lap, she waited.

Silent, Toby stared out over the waves. Their rhythmic movement back and forth like the deep breath from a barrel chest in slumber.

She followed his gaze to the long lines of reflected light dancing across the surface. The shimmering sea blurred the reflection, softening the streaks, making life seem a little less harsh. This place, the island of Coronado, was truly beautiful, a small piece of paradise. The reflected illumination from the curved bridge rose to the left, while the occasional horn honked, indicating traffic in the distance. However, for the moment, she could imagine in the tranquil silence, they had the isle all to themselves.

Toby took a breath. "There's the three of us kids," he said, his voice methodical, deep in thought. "My brother, then Carrie, and me. We lost Da too soon. He was a fisherman who died at sea. Ma did her best, but with Da gone, Carrie took it hardest. She was Daddy's girl, you see."

Wendee nodded, wondering what it would have been like to be Daddy's girl—or anybody's girl, for that matter. Toby's voice had hardened from its normal honeyed tones, and she braced. His face had taken on a faraway look and, though his lips moved, she doubted he sat with her in his mind. The past had claimed him, and he no longer resided on the island.

"But she was graduating—with honors. The first in the family to have been accepted to University with a scholarship. Sure, Bobby was away at college, but not with honors. Despite her grief, Ma wanted her to take part in the festivities. You're only young once, Ma always said. A few of her friends came by to get Carrie for the grad party. There were chaperones, but booze was a given."

Wendee's heart kicked up a notch with the mention of booze. She visualized the scene, remembering when she was a teenager. Trying so hard to fit in, to belong, while residing on the fringe. Risking rebuke, Wendee lifted her other hand to stroke the top of his and encourage him to continue when he stalled.

He laced his fingers with hers and squeezed. "I was there, too," he said. "But she was with her friends, and I was with mine. I never…it never occurred to me…I should have…jealousy creates a rage in some people. I didn't know there was past abuse…she never said…I couldn't imagine…how could she have kept such secrets?"

There were no answers. He didn't expect any. Wendee squeezed her eyes shut, terrified of what he was about to say. His voice no longer travelled through her ears but ebbed into her veins, impacting her central nervous system with the anticipation of what was to come. Intense dread combined with the need to know. With a direct hit to her heart, every syllable mattered. Despite her anxiety, she needed him to continue for his own sake. This had obviously been weighing him down for a long time.

"Then the police were called…the ambulance arrived. I was wasted, totally blotto with booze and the high of graduating. I didn't even know what was going on until my buddy, Mack, grabbed me to tell me my mom had crashed the party. Totally freaked out, I stumbled around, and then I saw her…Carrie, in the ambulance. Her face was purple with bruising, one eye almost closed, looking like an Easter egg. I turned away. I couldn't believe what I saw."

Toby swiped away a tear that leaked down his cheeks. "How long from when it happened to when I stumbled onto the scene, I couldn't say, but it must have been forever because then Ma came running, screaming."

Her two hands squeezed his, sandwiched between.

Time stretched. She wanted him to be done. His shoulders slumped, yet his legs tensed next to hers as though preparing for a sprint. She didn't want to ask. Wendee needed the story to end there. Yet... "What happened?" Wendee heard her voice come out as a croak.

He turned his gaze on her, his silvery eyes awash in a puddle, unshed. "We knew all three of them. Three! My God, three of them attacked my sister, who had never done anything to anyone." His voice was harsh. "The town is not so big. They were schoolmates, for Christ's sake, and what they did to my sister was...unforgivable."

"My God, Toby," Wendee whispered, covering her mouth with trembling fingers. She knew without being told. She didn't want the details and couldn't bear the pain, the tragedy, the horror. "I'm so sorry. She died from what they did? You couldn't have known. This couldn't possibly be your fault."

He shook his head and placed his palm against his forehead to scrub across his brow in what struck her as an effort to erase the memory. He lowered his hands and squeezed them together, turning them this way and that as though they provided answers. He folded one fist inside the other and lowered them to his lap. "Might as well have."

His breath raged shakily in and out several times. A vein throbbed in his temple, the blue accented by the paleness of his profile. Wendee kept her palm on his thigh, reassuring. His muscles rippled beneath her fingertips. Her leg muscles tensed, poised for flight. But she willed herself to stay put.

"I've asked myself for years, why? Why Carrie?

What did she ever do to them? But I'll never know. They were acquitted of the rape—judge said because everyone was drinking there was no criminal intent. Huh." He barked a laugh. "But that wasn't good enough for them, no. They took pictures."

"No," her voice hissed. Toby didn't appear to notice, and she was grateful. As he fell into silence, her imagination filled the gaps of his words. How could they? An innocent girl of only eighteen not only violated violently, her humiliation exposed for all to see.

After a while, Toby shook his head. "Taunted her with them. Threatened her if she said anything, they'd do it again." He banged his clenched fists against his thighs, and then stared up to the sky. "If they could get away with it once, what was to stop them?" He stopped talking and glowered.

His face was a thin-lipped mask Wendee didn't recognize. Fierce and hard, he had lost the usual kindness that made his jaw seem less squared. The reddish stubble cast a golden glow rather than shadow over his chin, and his jaw clenched and unclenched with the gnashing of his teeth. The pronounced cheekbones only served to accentuate the ice of his eyes. A jagged scar tracked along his hairline in front of his ear that she had never noticed before. She longed to run a finger along its edge. Yet, somehow, she knew the scar was part of the story.

"She committed suicide on March fourth. I killed the ringleader the same night...the other two were injured, but they lived. Being so close to eighteen, having been a boxer for many years, earning championship belts, I was tried as an adult. They said my actions were premeditated. My hands were weapons." A sob scratched up his throat. "I didn't even get to attend the funeral. No acquittal for me. I guess I wasn't in my right mind." His lips twitched and a smile widened to spread across his face. The smile was ironic, lacking any mirth. "Ma hired the best lawyer she could afford. My brother, Bobby, was always interested in law and used his connections from school. They were trying for an appeal when…"

"When?" Wendee prompted. He was silent so long, she wondered whether to repeat the question.

"It was too late for me."

Wendee's heart raced and struggled to contain the tears that threatened to flow. She couldn't tear her gaze from his face. This was not the man she had come to know these last weeks. This man who clenched his hands as though to hold back a monster looked more than capable of doing murder. Yet, she wasn't afraid. She blinked several times and strived to gain control over her breathing. "How did you make it here?" she asked at last.

"The legal system is a slow wheel. Served two years." He shook his head and laughed. "That was pleasant."

Wendee didn't see the humor and, by the look of his face, neither did Toby.

"I know now, they at least did me a kindness based on my age to send me to minimum security, instead of the hard core prison where murderers typically go."

"Ohmygod." The words jumbled as one.

"God had little to do with it." He tossed her a quick glance before turning his attention back to the ocean. "When a gang decided to make a run for it…well, here

I am."

"Alone?" Wendee twisted to look at him.

He smiled down at her and, for the first time, his eyes reflected a bit of mirth. "When prisoners escape, they don't typically stay together."

"I guess," she said, weakly. The whole idea rocked her.

"Bunch of guys I sparred with…not much else to do in the endless hours of waiting. If they were going to imprison me for weapons for hands, I felt the least I could do was train."

Again, he laughed. "What better training ground than prison?"

Wendee couldn't speak and felt her breath clog in her throat.

"Good thing I'm a big guy. I was shitting bricks my first night."

A tremor raced along her arms, and her palm danced off his thigh.

He picked up her hand and laced her fingers with his. "It was okay. I was fine," he said and squeezed her hand. "Da brought us up tough."

"Huh." The single word was all she managed.

"I was so filled with rage, Wendee. I was waiting for someone to make a move, and when they did…well, I didn't have any more problems."

"Oh, Toby."

Toby stroked back her hair from her face.

His features had returned to what she considered normal, and sympathy colored his gaze.

"As soon as we made it outside the compound, they dropped me like a hot potato. Didn't want some kid slowing them down."

"Was that a good thing?"

He shrugged. "I had to see Ma and tell her I was sorry. They couldn't change my mind. I might have been young, but I could hold my own."

Wendee didn't want to imagine what holding his own meant for a young man in prison. Rage or no. She had lost the battle with the tears, feeling them spring from the confines of her eyes to run down her cheeks.

"Said I was crazy for going home. That'd be the first place the police, or anyone, would look." He sighed, the sound hollow through his broad chest. "They were right, of course. Home was exactly where the police searched for me, but I didn't care. I had to see that Ma was okay. Within a year, she'd lost my Da, Carrie, and then me. All she had left was Bobby—Robert. I wonder if he ever became a lawyer like he wanted...I hope so."

He shrugged again, seeming reminiscent, and cradled her hand within his own. His thumb traced a circle on the inside of her wrist. "I didn't want to put them in any danger or cause more trouble...but I had to go to them."

"I understand." Wendee remembered losing her mother and having a father who couldn't care less. Then her grandmother, doing the very best she could, trying to be both. Even in reduced health, Nan was all she had and, despite Roger being able to track her, she understood the risk Toby had taken and the need for the contact. Wasn't she doing just that with her correspondence to Nan?

"Bobby knew I'd come home," Toby said after a brief pause. "When the police contacted him after the break from the penitentiary and he heard I was gone, he knew. He went straight to Ma. It was as though they knew I would try to escape and had been planning for it since I went behind bars. Between the two of them, I was smuggled out of town, onto a trawler, and out of the country."

"Are you serious? Just like that?"

He nodded. "Just like that. But we hit a storm. The fishermen thought they dropped me in Mexico. When we could see the light of the coast through the sheets of rain, I went over the side. Seems I missed the mark by a little when I swam here."

"You swam?"

"Yup." He pointed over the purple horizon. "From there."

Chapter Twelve

Toby stared down at their linked fingers, resting atop his thigh. At last, the sounds from the marina, sea birds, and general population reached him. With an awareness of his surroundings, he felt as though he had returned from a long journey. He was tired and drained. Pulling air in through his nose, he braced himself to glance at his companion.

She smiled. Moisture clung to the tips of her eyelashes.

He reached a thumb to run across her cheek, and a lightness of spirit filled him as he gazed into Wendee's warm eyes. He swallowed back the lump in his throat. She hadn't rejected him, fled in outrage, or condemned him. Instead, she held his hand and sat in silence, looking over the ocean while the night had passed.

She squeezed his fingers and rested her head against his shoulder. "Where's home?"

He stiffened, the mistrust of giving away too much firming his spine. When she lifted her head and glanced up at him, he shrugged. "Old habit."

"I get it," she said, and shrugged before turning her gaze back to the marina. "You don't have to tell me."

He sighed. "North. Up the Pacific coast, into Canada."

"British Columbia?"

He nodded. "Yup. Toward Alaska—Prince

Rupert."

"Never been." She shook her head. "'Course, I've never been to a lot of places."

"Me either, really." He smiled as familiar faces and places from his memories flooded into recollection. "But I didn't really have any ambition to. Home is beautiful—rugged, untamed—the people are tough."

Her fingers stroked his forearm. "Like you?"

The warmth of her touch thrilled along his nerve endings. Toby laughed, imagining what some of those salty fishermen he grew up with would think of him now. "No." He shook his head. "They'd call me soft."

Wendee sat up, dropped his hand, and twisted to face him. "There is nothing soft about standing up for someone you love and standing by your integrity. If there were more men in the world who—"

"People lost their lives." Toby looked down at his legs, feet crossed at the ankles. He laced his fingers together and rested them on his lap. "There is no integrity in what I did. I have to live with the consequences of my actions. I played police, judge, and jury. Took me a long time to realize that."

"We could only hope to have someone like you on our side for all of those who suffered what those thugs did to your sister," Wendee shot back, and her eyes flashed. "Tell me, if you had it to do over again...would you do anything differently?"

Silence sat between them like a wall. In his mind's eye, he saw his sister, Carrie, as she had been when they were children. Then her normally clever features and quirky smile, alight with teasing, vanished behind the pale features of a stranger whose very essence was stolen away without permission. He curled his fingers into a fist. The crunch of his knuckles popping gave away the intensity of his emotional response. The raw impact of his rage struck like a blow to the gut. A white heat swept across his brow as he relived his complete ineptitude to help Carrie when she needed him most. Toby unlocked his ankles, bending his legs to sit forward, releasing his fists with effort to balance his elbows on his knees. His shoulders tightened, and he rubbed his palms along his upper legs, curbing the urge to lash out, or stand and run.

His response struck a heavy blow. The façade of calm he struggled to hone these last years crumbled with her single question. He couldn't outrun what had been done to his sister. Nor could he outrun his continued reaction. "No." He pounded his bunched hands on the wood slats of the bench. "Goddamn me to hell, I'd do it again."

"Despite what you know now?" Wendee's voice probed, unrelenting.

He cast a glance sideways to view her profile. She sat stiff beside him, obstinate in her position. Strong. She was no coward. Unafraid, she stared back, gaze steady. She blinked rapidly and color heightened her cheeks, yet she retained the space between them.

With one quick move, she breached the distance with a light touch to his bicep. "Being hunted down—on the run—facing the exile from your family…friends…everything you knew?"

He forced his hands to open only to curl his palms around the edge of the wooden seat. Shoulders sagged, he hung his head between his shoulders, and he shook it back and forth, trying to understand. "Why are you asking me this?" The words scratched like sandpaper across his throat. A foot tucked under the bench as though on the runner's block, awaiting the firing gun. He leaned forward to try to encapsulate the hurt. "I opened myself to you. I have told you things I never told anyone before." The breath of freedom he felt earlier with the purging of his soul had vanished. He paused, shrugged his shoulders and sighed with a shaky flutter to the air he drew. He was ashamed he'd revealed so much. He thought he had grown, matured, and paid his dues. "I don't know why I—"

Her hand encircled his upper arm and squeezed. "Because, right or wrong, Toby, you'd do it again."

Her voice came closer. The hair on his forearms stood up as if reaching to touch her. He heard her draw breath.

"It's not for me to judge you. I wasn't there. I can't possibly know. But from what you've told me, I can guess your sister would never judge you as harshly as you do yourself. You live the life of a monk. You have closed yourself off from other people. You're a good man." The feather light touch of her lips flicked across his ear. Her voice softened to a whisper. "But you've allowed me to get to know you now, and I can tell you this…I'd want you there for me."

Toby turned slightly to see her. She had closed the gap between them again, snuggling against his side. Her eyes swam in the pre-dawn light. He raised his palm to cup her cheek. His thumb ran along the line of her lips, and she kissed the tip.

"I'd be there for you," he said.

Toby wanted to ask her about her story. He wanted to care for her. Now that he'd opened his heart and exposed his weakness, and she didn't condemn him, he wanted more. The lightness was back. For the first time in a long time, perhaps ever, gazing into the melted toffee of her eyes, a future felt possible. With his heart thunking against his ribcage, he unfolded his hands and reached for her.

She wrapped her arms about his neck and leaned in until their noses touched. Her gaze penetrated through to his soul. "Take me home."

Toby folded his hands over her shoulders, stroking her neck with his fingers. "I can't go back."

She rubbed his nose, Eskimo style, and her eyes crinkled with mirth. Tears rolled down the side of her face. "Here," she said, and leaned her head to indicate the marina. "Your houseboat."

Toby pulled back. "How do you know..."

"You're not the only one who stalks."

****

Toby dropped her hand to jump onto the deck of the boat. Turning back, he gathered Wendee into his arms and lifted her down. When she twined her fingers in his hair and nuzzled his neck, he thought his knees might buckle. Instead of releasing her, he strode the few feet to the door with her cradled against his chest. Holding her close, his body stiff with wanting, he freed a hand to twist the knob, not needing a key because he never locked it. With his backside toward the opening, he sidestepped through and strode directly to the bedroom.

Her hands had snaked their way under his shirt, and her fingers fanned across his chest, while her mouth continued an exploration across his shoulders. By the time he laid her gently on the coverlet, his breath had turned to gasps.

Wendee wiggled into the center of the bed. "Still don't do this?"

The sound of her voice flowed through his ears and settled in his loins. He ached, and a sudden laugh erupted to emerge from the depths of his lungs like a bark. He kicked off his shoes and knelt on the bed, palms flattened on either side of her hips. "I do now." He bent to cover her lips with his. Like a flower, she opened to him; the scent of her filled his senses. The warmth of her body filled the cold recesses of his soul, making him feel whole again. Her arms wrapped around his waist and her tongue flicked out to stroke his. When she arched toward him, he lightly traced his fingers along her silky sides.

Squirming under him, she broke the kiss and stretched to remove her shirt.

Toby reached to still her hand. "No."

"No?"

If this were her gift to him, he would savor the moment. No one knew better than he how fleeting these instances could be. "Allow me."

She shook her head, and her body ground up against his. "I want you...now."

He smiled with what he hoped would convince the rest of his body to be patient. Despite his passion making itself known, he chuckled, the sound emerging as it should. "I almost lost my job because of you today," he said, his hands molding around her breasts, thumbs rubbing across the raised buds of her nipples.

"Do you have any idea..." His fingers fluttered against her stomach and inched up her shirt. With the same slow movements he used on his patients, he lifted her blouse. "...how hard..." One by one, he released the buttons to expose the creamy skin. His lips followed the path, up over the boundary of her bra until he reached her neck. "...it was to keep a professional distance?" Where his fingers would normally massage, his lips kissed and his tongue tasted.

She bowed her back to grant him access. He wanted nothing more than to rush, but he wouldn't allow himself. Shackles that had held him back for so long had finally freed him.

"Toby," she moaned, the sound searing his soul. Her hands fisted in the corner of the pillows. "No distance."

He wouldn't hurry now, no matter what. To rush would be to miss the moments, and the way this woman squirmed and yearned for him was like a magic wand suddenly striking him alive.

His teeth nipped her lips before he covered her mouth with his, reaching to her shoulders to lower the bra straps. When she arched, he stretched behind her back and fumbled until the latch of lingerie released. Slow deliberation measured his movements and he lifted to watch her response, captivated while he guided the straps over her shoulders until the mounds were exposed. He inched down to draw first one, then the other taut nipple between his lips. How had he lived so long never experiencing the taste of a woman in his mouth? Then, in one swift motion, he tossed aside his T-shirt.

Wendee raised her legs to wrap around his waist. Moving her hips in a circular motion, she ground her pelvis to his.

While his mouth wrought fiery tingles singing along her nerve endings, his fingers splayed over her stomach, teasing under her waistline. With his thumb and forefinger, he released the button. She dropped her feet to the bed and allowed him to push down the garment over her hips. Flicking his tongue across her navel, he worked his way back up her body, savoring her flavor, her smell, the very essence. The unique feminine scent heightened his sense of awareness of her, along with the soft mewing of her response to his touch. Kicking off his shorts, he drew up beside her, his hand wrapping around her neck to pull her against him.

Every nerve ending seemed to sing out, rejoicing yet demanding more. With each kiss—caress—her body brought his alive for the first time. He cupped her hips, and reared up. "You are so beautiful."

She sat up so her hands could splay across his chest and follow the line of hair down his navel until her fingers stroked his penis.

His legs quivered with restraint. He didn't know how much longer he could hold back.

As she folded her palm to cup his testicles, her fingers creating a zest of new feelings, she said, "You are beautiful—every glorious inch."

He never expected to hear such things said about him. He leaned forward and chuckled, spell momentarily broken. His hands braced on her hips, he continued forward until his lips touched hers. Then he pulled back. "Boys aren't beautiful."

Her fingers wound through the damp curls of his hair. "You're no boy. And you most certainly are." She spread her legs and guided him toward her apex.

Chapter Thirteen

Between the sway of the boat and being curled in a lover's arms, Wendee felt more secure than she had ever in her life previously. With Toby's trust in her, she felt she could finally be the person she wanted to be, not a reflection of the person she left behind or the woman she had to be to survive in Minnesota. California had offered a fresh start, a new beginning, and after this time with Toby, she would have to find some way to make the new start last. Whatever came, perhaps with Toby by her side, she could make a go of things here—make everything work out.

A firm shake of her head put thoughts of Roger back into the compartment where, for months, she'd housed all fear of him finding her.

Toby's grip tightened around her waist. "Everything okay?" Voice husky, his breath tickled the hollow of her neck.

Wendee wiggled her backside closer to snuggle. She sighed then smiled with his instant reaction to her proximity. "For someone who doesn—"

"I do..." Toby's teeth nipped her ear. "With you..." He growled, the sound of a man content. He moved his lips down her neck. "I absolutely do."

As his hands explored her body, Wendee melted into his touch. "And I am so glad you do."

The next while passed in the continued discovery

of one another's bodies. Finally, Wendee stretched, her muscles like jelly. "Who would ever need a massage after that?"

Toby rolled to the side of the bed then stood. Turning his head, he smiled down at her. "That"—he lifted his chin toward her—"would take a lot longer than sixty minutes, and I don't think it would ever make the 'menu of services' in the spa."

Wendee giggled. "Let's keep it between the two of us, then."

"Our secret?"

She threw her knee over the sheets and rested her head on her hand. "Definitely our secret."

"Hungry?" he asked.

"You cook?"

"Some."

He bent to retrieve his shorts, and Wendee admired the firm roundness of his backside, her insides alive and tingling for more of his touch. The muscles of his back rippled as he straightened. His hair, mussed and untethered, floated in waves about his shoulders. He ran his fingers through the curls, got caught on a tangle, and shook his fingers free, tossing her a smile as he moved from the room.

"Ummm," she sighed. Wendee gathered her clothes and stepped into the small shower. From what she had seen of the houseboat: the bedroom and now the bathroom, Toby kept a neat and tidy place. Impressive, considering he hadn't expected company. Refreshed, she stepped from the small room only to be enveloped with the aroma of fresh coffee, eggs, bacon, and buttered toast. She loved the smell of toast. Her favorite.

She finger-brushed her short hair and tucked the sides behind her ears as she made her way aft. "You cook," she repeated, unable to keep the surprise from her voice. He continued to impress her in every way.

He turned, his smile broadening, crinkling his eyes. The silvery gaze swept down her body, then back up, leaving a ripple of tingles in their wake. He stepped toward her, closing the gap between them with a single stride. His hands braced against her shoulders, and he bent his head. He breathed in audibly through his nose. "You smell so good. I thought maybe it was a soap you use. But, no." He tilted back his head to nod. "It's all you."

A rush of pleasure flushed her body from her core to color her face. No one had ever spoken to her in such a way where she felt the words rather than just heard them. Each syllable radiated along her nerve endings. She reached to frame his face with her hands. She rubbed her nose gently against his, and then kissed his lips. The stubble above his mouth tickled, standing in sharp contrast to the silky smoothness of his lips. His touch left her wanting to invite him back to the bedroom. Yet, the smell of breakfast made her stomach growl.

Toby pulled back and chuckled. "Worked up an appetite, I see. Better get you fed."

"What time's your shift today?"

He glanced at the clock on the wall above the sink. "Later. How about you?"

Adopting his casual manner, she sat at the table, folded a leg under her bum, and admired the simple setting. "Later, too," she replied.

He set the plate of food before her, complete with

an orange garnish.

Wendee waited for him to sit. She reached for her napkin and spread it across her knee, leaned forward, and smelled the wonderful combination of food.

"Dig in," he said, lifting his chin. He picked up his fork to tuck into the eggs. "Before it gets cold."

She followed his lead and enjoyed every bite. Wiping the corners of her mouth, she sat back on her chair. "You can cook."

With an elbow on the table, he rested his head in a hand. "That's three times you said that." He smiled. "I live alone. If I didn't cook, I wouldn't eat."

Wendee shook her head. "Plenty of guys live alone, and they can't cook. I've been told that's what fast food is for. That, or they open a box or a can. But you can cook." Feeling the frisky side he always drew out in her return, she locked her gaze with his. "A man of many talents."

Color brushed across his cheeks, and his gaze dropped to his plate before returning to her. "Thank you."

****

Holding her hand the whole way, Toby walked Wendee back to her place. "Too bad Evangeline isn't home," Wendee said at her gate. "I'd love for you to meet her."

"You're lucky to have family." A glint of sadness deepened the gray of his eyes despite the smile he bestowed upon her.

"I am," Wendee agreed. "To think I went so long where it was just Nan and I."

Toby reached for her other hand. "Will you tell me more about your family? Your grandmother? I can see she's important to you."

If he could reveal his deepest secrets, surely anything she had to say would be fine. When she hesitated, he swung her hands gently. "It's okay," he cooed.

He didn't look hurt. His face reflected a warm patience. She felt she could take her time, and he'd understand. He confirmed this with his next words.

"All in your own time. Can I see you again tonight?"

She smiled and squeezed his hands. "Will you feed me?"

He grinned, the light returning to his eyes. "Of course."

"I get off at eleven."

He bent forward to kiss her full on the mouth, his tongue swiping across her lips, gaining access.

Wendee bowed into him—melting, toes curling, feeling the draw from deep in her core.

He released her, hands braced against her hips, and held her until she steadied herself. He smiled a knowing smile, eyes crinkled at the edge. "I know where you work."

****

Wendee sat for a long while at the window seat overlooking the ocean. What would she do? Where would she go now? What she wanted to do warred with what her practical mind told her she should do. In the heat of the moment with Toby, she had been stupid to allow herself to think she could stay. She had no experience with being on the run. No idea how to hide effectively. How long did she have before Roger found her?

Could she trust Toby like he confided in her? A part of her longed to believe, but knowing what she knew about him, she couldn't put him in a position where he would once again be held to task for another's actions. If he came face to face with Roger...if he chose to step in...she couldn't chance placing him in that kind of dangerous position.

Especially now that she understood his history, she couldn't risk telling him how she had inadvertently gotten involved in a mob operation, and they somehow thought she had made off with millions of their dollars and were now hunting her down. He was the kind of guy who would do something. She had asked him, would he do it again.

Wendee leaned her forehead against the glass. When Roger and his men found her without the money, would they kill her? Her stomach tightened, and her throat closed. She struggled for breath. For as long as she had been on the island, she had managed to delude herself to the extent of the seriousness of her situation. This was partly due to the fact that she simply couldn't believe it was happening. And now...there was Eva, there was Toby.

Without a doubt, she had to leave. Now. She couldn't bring herself to tell Eva or anyone she had gotten close to these last months. She didn't want to draw them into her situation. The last thing she wanted was to have them involved. At this time, she could only guess that Roger merely had knowledge of where she worked, not where she lived. For now, the people she loved—

Love?

Yes, she loved Eva. Of course. They were family.

However many years between their visits, they had a connection. In her cousin, she had found a sister she never had—a best friend who seemed to understand her without Wendee ever having to say anything. Eva didn't push her, even though she was no dummy when it came to Wendee just popping up one day out of the blue.

How about Toby? A warmth flooded her veins and filled all the secret spots she revealed to no one. Love? One night together didn't amount to love.

Or did it?

She certainly had never felt this way before. Such an intense draw to another person. A deep kindness, an affection. She cared what happened to him. She was moved by his bravery, his tenacity to live, his willingness to fight—

Precisely why she had to go.

Love or not, after hearing about his sister, Carrie, Wendee cared enough to not want to put him in another situation where he would have to flee again. Vigilante justice never worked. Whether he realized it or not, he had built a home here on the island of Coronado. If there was some way for him to contact his family and let them know he was okay…maybe…

The front door squeaked then the screen door banged shut, announcing Eva's return from her day at the office. Wendee checked her watch. Eva was off early tonight. The woman worked all hours, and sometimes Wendee went a couple of days without crossing paths.

Eva peeked around the corner from the kitchen, brows raised in question. "I thought you'd be at work."

"I didn't think you'd be home for hours." Wendee

hugged her knees to her chest, chin resting on top.

Eva's blonde hair was laced back in a loose braid to hang across her shoulder. With little to no makeup, Wendee had been around her cousin long enough now to know Eva had no idea of her causal beauty. Wendee assumed the slight exotic slant to her eyes came from her grandmother's Trinidadian descent. Everything else epitomized the California girl.

Eva sighed, hand braced against the wall. "I'm just done-in today. I honestly couldn't take one…more…phone…call."

"How I understand. I'm off for my shift in a bit," Wendee replied, releasing her hold on her knees. She straightened her legs and stretched like a cat in the sunshine. She glanced back out to the sea. "Truly. Eva, you have the best spot on the island. I got the wrong set of grandparents," Wendee said without rancor.

"Aunty Maribel is simply the best person I ever knew," Eva replied. "Grande Papere Reggie always spoke of her strength of character as something all of us should aspire to."

Remembering her treasured times with her Nana, Wendee blinked back a tear at the loss. "She was—is," she corrected, remembering though her Nan was in decline, she wasn't dead. After a moment of silence, she smiled and patted the nautical blue cushion upon which she sat. "She always spoke about the fortune of having the love of a good man…but she lacked the real estate."

Eva walked to Wendee and plopped down beside her. She wrapped her arms around Wendee, drawing her back against her while they gazed out over the golden sands of the beachfront. "Grande Papere says the very same thing. You have to remember, he and Aunty Maribel grew up in a house without love. There was only ambition. When he and Nanny Elleah met on this very island, he gained the strength to free Aunty Maribel from that asylum. He helped her find your mother—who had been snatched from her without consent—and start again when her father continued to disown her."

"She surrounded us with so much love and built a life without the bonds of the family money." Wendee sighed. "Makes you wonder why Mama would go down the road she did."

"It's not for me to judge," Eva replied, strengthening her embrace. "My mother, the starlet, and my brother, the rock star. I can't compete, so sometimes I feel I don't exist. I tried for so long to live up to their super stardom, but really, this is where I'm most comfortable. Behind the scenes."

"Helping the mega rich continue to be mega-rich and associate with other one-percenters."

"Yes...no." Eva chuckled. "Spend some of their riches and maybe make a bit, as well. Be self-supporting. Create some lasting happiness."

"Hobnob with the rich and famous. You know anyone who's anyone."

Eva shook her head and hugged Wendee tighter. "They don't even know who I am, other than a voice on the other end of the phone. I swear they'd never know me if I walked right up to any of them." She paused and laughed again. "In actual fact, they'd likely walk the other way. These ultra-diva personalities would never want to admit they had to use someone like me to make it onto the red carpet. I simply relate people through connections. All to their mutual gain."

"Or so you convince them," Wendee said, the bud of an idea building.

"That's the job," Eva replied, giving Wendee one last squeeze before gaining her feet. "Not much different than you at the Del. Working the front desk, isn't it your job to ensure people have what they requested? When the concierge isn't there, you do it. You've come home plenty of times with stories of getting upgrades and the like."

Wendee stood, as well. "But only within the hotel."

"Same thing," Eva said.

Eva spoke as Wendee imagined a sister would.

"I use what I know and go from there," Eva continued.

Whatever Eva had, she'd more than earned. How some man hadn't scooped up her cousin was a mystery. Wendee swallowed the sudden lump. "I'm so glad we found each other again."

"Me, too." Eva brushed a hand over Wendee's arm before turning to walk back to the kitchen. "If I hadn't decided to move down from San Francisco instead of going to New York, who knows if our paths would have ever met again."

Wondering about Roger, Wendee pondered if that would have been better.

Chapter Fourteen

Toby adjusted the checked cloth, and then tucked the picnic basket out of sight behind the pillar next to the chairs across from the front desk in the foyer of the hotel. After his shift ended, he splurged on wine and some of his favorite delicacies from the open-air market off Ocean Avenue. Tonight, he would take Wendee to his spot by the lighthouse. He wanted to share everything he loved about the island. Anticipation thrilled through his blood. He wanted her to feel comfortable enough to share with him. Mostly, he wanted to be worthy enough for her to feel that she could share. Being with Wendee finally allowed Toby the opportunity to face his past and, perhaps, move forward.

Perhaps.

To his mind, whatever she had run from couldn't have been too bad if she was still in contact with her family. But, everyone had their cross to bear. Far be it for Toby to judge. However, he felt now, anything could be overcome so long as they were together. That she wanted to be with him seemed a miracle unto itself. At last, he felt worthy of someone else's love.

Love?

He pondered the concept.

Could it be possible? So soon?

But really, what did time matter when it came to a

connection with another person?

Toby chewed his lip. No, he wouldn't dissect the feelings he was experiencing. He would simply allow himself the small indulgence of gratification in the moment.

Leaning against the pillar, pleasure at watching Wendee finish up with some late check-ins coursed through him, making him grin. His jaw was sure to ache from smiling all the time, but he didn't care. Even today, the ladies in the spa had noted the difference in him. He caught them nudging one another and whispering whenever he walked by. He shrugged. Life, he realized, was no life alone. He wanted Wendee with all his being. Was this love? He placed a hand over his chest and felt the thump of his heart. Yes. He glanced across to her. Her smile radiated through to his soul. She made him feel things he never imagined would be possible for him again.

He brushed a hand through his hair and recalled their night together. He understood he was forever changed. The silk of her skin under his palms. The sheen of perspiration that made her glow in the moonlight through the port window. The scent of their union. Is this what it is to be reborn? Start fresh? Begin anew? Though she could never take away or make him forget his actions, somehow the sharing had lessened the load he hadn't realized had become so heavy all these years. For the first time, he even considered trying to make contact with his family. Surely, there could be second chances even for a man like him.

Toby ached to find out more about her. The slight sadness hidden in the depths of her eyes. The way she would look to the horizon, lost within herself. Where was she from? During their time together, she had indicated the Midwest, but where? What of the rest of her family? He knew she lived with her cousin and had an ailing grandmother, but what about her parents? Who had scared her enough to abandon her life before California?

More importantly, who had hurt her, and how? He rubbed the tips of his fingers, remembering the scars on her back, the way she winced when his palms glided across their surface. She didn't want to talk about her past, her parents, none of it. Toby understood. He respected her decision, but that didn't take away his concern.

Toby felt his hands curl into fists and looked down willing his fingers to splay apart. Violence was not the answer. Never again. Yet, the yearning remained. But he longed to protect her—still, there were other ways and they would find them—together. The first was to get her to trust him.

He drew his thoughts from the past and returned to the present, glancing to the counter.

As though sensing him, her head rose from her task, and she scanned the foyer. Her chin came up, and a smile lifted her cheeks when she spotted him. Her hand skimmed her hair, flattening a wayward wisp. She scooped it behind her ear.

How could a woman look so sexy in such a basic uniform? Yet, the burgundy vest over the short-sleeved khaki shirt, complemented by the striped tie, made her amber eyes glow and her skin radiate. Her short hair shuffled into a side part, spiked around her crown, gave her an impish air. The way she had taunted him these last weeks gave Toby no doubt the mischievous manner was more than a look. An attitude to life, more like.

Gooseflesh coursed along his arms. He checked the magnificent grandfather clock across the foyer. Impatient until he could be with Wendee again, Toby twisted from the wall to gather the basket. Just about time for her shift to end and be on their way. When he stood, his gaze caught a glint from a flash of silver reflected in the overhead lighting. *What the ...*

A square-jawed man, as wide across the shoulders as he was tall, stood behind an elderly couple, an official-looking badge held in the palm of his hand, poised at the ready.

Toby's hackles rose, and the muscles of his legs tensed, readying for flight. But he willed his body to still. By Toby's estimation, the man would be considered plain-clothed, but the officer—if that is what he was—was anything but ordinary. He certainly didn't fit in with the casual attire of the people filtering through the lobby of the Del.

His suit jacket stretched across his back, and his free hand braced against his hip. The man tapped his foot with an impatient manner.

Toby's stomach clenched, bile rising as the policeman approached the front desk. Heart hammering and breath lodged in his throat, Toby moved closer to the wall, into the shadows. Swiping a palm across his forehead, he wiped away the dew of perspiration. He'd seen plenty of police since living on the island. Hell, he'd treated many for their aches and pains, along with the local military guys. Surely, he had nothing to be concerned about after all this time. Yet, whether from the revelation of the night before tossing everything to the surface again, or premonition, he couldn't contain the sudden nausea assaulting his gut.

Five after eleven. No, he shook his head. This would have nothing to do with him. He scanned the area for Wendee, but she must have already gone to gather her things.

He swallowed hard, adjusted the basket in his hand, and forced himself to stride across the lobby. Toby nodded at Calvin, who tossed him the briefest of glances before turning his attention to the officer who reminded Toby of a large rectangle. Everything, including the man's deeply sunken eyes, looked to be formed by right angles.

Toby leaned to peer around the wall to the side of the desk. Wendee disappeared, as had the swarm of guests from just before. A nervous twitch bounced in Toby's cheek when it seemed as though only the three of them remained in the lobby. Where had Wendee gone? She knew he waited for her to be done for the night. Though they hadn't planned anything official, she must know he had come for her.

The officer turned to Toby. "I'm Detective Clark Kingston, out of Minneapolis. Have you seen this woman?" He held a wallet-sized picture, creased and battered by handling. "I believe she goes by the name Cavanaugh."

The photo portrayed a woman from the shoulders up, long brown hair with a slight wave who wore glasses. Even the thick, dark rims of the frames couldn't hide the heat those golden eyes created in him. "Cavanaugh?" Toby questioned, tightening his grip on the handle of the basket. "Sorry."

The policeman's eyes narrowed. He laid a palm on the counter, straight brows raised. "So nobody knows this woman?" the officer asked with a disbelieving air, trawling his penetrating gaze between Toby and Calvin. "What about the woman who shared this shift with you when I was waiting? Where is she now?"

Calvin shrugged. "Her shift ended at eleven. Maybe you should come back during regular hours and talk to management."

"I mean to," Kingston replied, his vocals seeming to have taken a mile to reach the surface. Guttural and intense, he commanded attention even in the pauses between the words. "I just arrived tonight and thought I would take a chance. Wrap this up faster and get back home, you know?"

Neither Toby nor Calvin responded. What could they say? Whatever *this* was, giving Wendee a few extra hours to plan and prepare could make all the difference.

The officer drummed his fingers on the marble-topped high desk, the random click of a nail creating an ominous rhythm. "And you? Don't you get off at eleven, as well? Where's the next shift? Maybe they know where I can find this woman."

Calvin shrugged. "Yeah, sure, I'm supposed to be off," he responded, two spots of color adorning his cheeks. "But our night auditor's been held up by a family situation. She'll be here by midnight. I stayed. I can use the overtime."

Kingston stretched his arm to check his watch. "I see." He resumed the drumming of his fingers and glanced at Toby, then down at the basket. He nodded, as though dismissing Toby as a guest and not an employee. Then he stepped back from the desk and folded his arms across his chest. "Go ahead."

Toby's stomach lurched as he locked eyes with Calvin. Neither was under any illusion as to the officer's intent to find Wendee, despite not asking what the officer wanted with her. Yet without words of collaboration, they were unwilling to participate. Toby side-stepped down to stand in front of Calvin, leaned forward, and placed his elbow on the counter, feigning a casual stance he didn't feel. He scrambled for something to say. "I—ah...I'd like to...ah...use the lounge chairs down on the beach," he fumbled, pointing with his chin toward the ocean. "The hotel won't have a problem with that?"

Lightning flashed and thunder followed closely on its heels. Toby glanced outside then down to his picnic basket. Shit.

Calvin reacted much quicker than Toby. The wide smile—Toby suspected for the benefit of the detective—didn't reach the clerk's eyes. "Bit of rain out there right now, looks like a storm brewing. So...maybe not the right night for it...but so long as there's no open liquor, the area's yours to use."

Toby nodded and moved back, said thank you before proceeding around the corner to the staff entrance. As he walked away, he overheard Calvin resume a halting conversation with Officer Kingston. If the policeman stubbornly held on until midnight, Toby was sure Wendee would be made. She wouldn't stand a chance. Toby had to find her now.

****

The lights of the long hallway flickered as though in tune with the nerves radiating throughout Wendee's body. Was this the actions of the ghost of Kate Morgan come to her rescue? Hadn't Kate been hunted, and then found dead by mysterious means? Fleetingly, Wendee wondered about the circumstances that resulted in a young woman, travelling alone, being found dead—murder or suicide—no one ever drew a conclusion.

Wendee shook her head and carried on. She didn't see much of the same romantic glamor in her own situation. She paused for breath when she reached the staff lounge. Going straight for the bathroom, she stood in the toilet cubicle and stared at the ceiling. In here, the fluorescent light strengthened, and Wendee squeezed her eyes closed, bracing her hands on either side of her head. There would be no one to come to her rescue. For years after her father's abandonment, because she lived with her grandmother, she adopted the Cavanaugh name as her own. She had somehow expected to be shielded from discovery by reverting to her real surname—Miller—because she didn't think Roger even knew of it. How stupid and inexperienced she had been throughout this entire endeavor.

Here, all this time, she had expected Roger to find her. Now, she had actually been discovered by the cops? They thought she was mob. Incredible. Had Roger turned the tables and reported her to the authorities. How? What would he have reported her for—theft? Wouldn't he have to explain how she stole the money and its origins?

Now she wished she had the forethought to steal the damned money. She would have gladly given it back and carried on her merry way. She'd have had leverage with the cash. Stealing never entered her thought pattern. Part of being a professional bookkeeper was making sure every cent added up. She loved the clarity the columns of numbers provided. She felt like a detective herself when something came up unbalanced and she was able to find it—fix the problem. "Fuck," she breathed out, the sound almost a moan.

Money. Millions of dollars missing. Everyone thought she was involved. Christ, if she had the cash, would she really be working the front desk at some hotel? No, she'd be stashed in the penthouse and certainly Nan would be with her.

A fit of hysterical giggles overcame her, and she covered her mouth to muffle the sound. Of course, she was running from a ghost of sorts, because there had never been any money. Yet, she couldn't prove her innocence to a bunch of thugs who had used her as scapegoat and certainly everything placed her at the scene for the cops. There was no winning this battle. She had to disappear, and for good this time. No more mistakes. She'd make sure Eva took care of Nan. Wendee could trust Eva.

She shook her head and swallowed back the sob that replaced the unhinged laughter bubbling up her throat. Her mind splintered in a million directions. She exited the stall and walked over to lock the main bathroom door. She didn't think she'd be bothered this time of night, but she needed a moment or two, and was in no condition to exchange small talk.

No, she couldn't outrun both the authorities and the mob. She couldn't turn herself in to the cops, either. For sure, Roger could falsify the books and make it look as though she were siphoning legitimate funds. Her fingers closed around the steel door handle. Their trembling made it hard to retain her grip. She lifted her hands to peer at them more closely, and then braced her palms against each other. Perhaps she should go out and face down whatever came her way. To delay only prolonged the inevitable. She leaned her ear against the door waiting for someone to shout her name, hailing her back to the front desk. Yet, all remained quiet.

Turning her back to the door, she returned to the sink. With precise movements, she washed then dried her hands before removing the vest and neck scarf. Folding them carefully, she placed them inside her backpack. Staring at the uniform, she made her decision. If she could make it back to Eva's, she would say goodbye and try to explain, begging forgiveness for placing her in such a situation. With the cops here, it wouldn't be long before they found Eva.

Wendee had never expected to become so close to her cousin, but that woman could hold her own. Eva was a marvel in every sense of the word—a treasured friend, family. Wendee wasn't worried, just ashamed. Had she joined the ranks of her father and become an embarrassment to the family?

On the topic of unexpected and family, there was Toby. Her esophagus clogged with emotion, and she swallowed hard. Bending, she cupped some water in her hand to sip and add much-needed moisture to her dry mouth. What would he think? Where was he now? He had been in the lobby when the officer approached. But he wouldn't be there now, she knew. He had survived too long to stick around. Obviously he, unlike her, knew what he was about in getting lost.

She raised her hands to her hot cheeks. The lights flickered again, and she recalled the mystery of Kate Morgan. "I understand you, Kate," Wendee whispered, closing her bag. "I'm all alone too." Flinging her bag over her shoulder, she squared her stance and opened the heavy wooden door.

She walked through the staff room to the entrance that led to the hallway. If she were careful, she could avoid being seen and take the rear exit toward the beach side of the hotel and slip away. If she darted to the water's edge, she could stay in the shadows and make it back to Eva's. Planning as she moved, she opened the door to peek out.

The door swung wide.

She gasped, and the lights went out.

Chapter Fifteen

"Come with me."

Wendee didn't hesitate when Toby's strong fingers laced with her own. The darkness was not complete. A faint glow from the torches outside on the boardwalk showed them the way to the exit.

With her heart in her mouth expecting the officer to give chase, Wendee felt as though the walls were closing in on her. Toby held her hand, pulling her close so her forearm sandwiched up to the side of his body, along his ribcage, forcing her to keep pace. Without running, they raced through the door at the end of the corridor and wound their way across the flagstones and onto the boardwalk. A light rain fell. A briefest glance at the horizon showed a storm brewing. Lightning, like electrified chain link, flashed upon the surface.

They avoided the circular illumination cast by the outside lights and kept to the shadows. He led her down across the damp sand toward the surf. She tripped several times on the uneven terrain, but she had no worry of falling. Toby held her safe. Lightning struck far out at sea, and the thunder crackled in the distance. Waves were already sweeping across the beach, covering their tracks.

Panting, she bumped into his solid form when he suddenly stopped. They hadn't been running, but she felt as though she'd just completed a sprint. He dropped whatever he had been holding and turned to her. With a swift, fluid motion, he pulled her to him, gripped her tight to his body while his lips claimed hers.

A fierce hunger consumed her. Would she ever experience these emotions again? Was this goodbye? Desperation took hold of the moment. Ravenous, she wound her fingers in his hair and pulled him close. Her tongue darted along his parted lips. He answered her body's request with a hand braced behind her head.

Within a moment, they were on their knees. The wet sand accommodated their every movement, swaying, parting, and cushioning where they needed. Wet from the rain, the wildness of the surf served only to fuel their passion, making each moment matter. Then he was on top of her, and she linked her arms around his neck. She moaned his name, and he growled, his lips trailing the edge of her jaw, along her throat, to the hollow of her shoulder. Within moments, her shirt was unbuttoned, and his fingers traced the curve of her body, dipping beneath the waistline of her shorts.

Frantic, knowing this might be the last time she would ever see this man, ever experience this kind of emotion, ever love in the way she loved him, she tore at his clothing. Soaked with the pelting rain, the fabric clung until she fervently ripped the cotton cloth from his body. She blinked back the tears, glad of the storm to hide her response to losing a love she never expected to find. Legs wrapped round his waist, she rolled so she lay on top and, shimmying down, unzipped his jeans. He threw aside his pants as she wiggled out of her shorts. Thunder boomed, and she clung to him.

He cupped her face. "You are so beautiful, Wendee." He rolled her again, so he hovered above, sheltering her from the deluge. "I never imagined..." He claimed her mouth, and she arched up to welcome his thrusts. Adding punctuation to his words, he filled her, balanced with an elbow on the sand, his palm next to her cheek, while his other hand gripped her hip. "You mean everything to me." Slowly, he moved and she tilted her head, her fingers splayed across his lower back.

Toby's tongue licked the moisture from her throat while he filled her again, and she anchored her legs around his middle, holding him close. "I want you so badly," he moaned, moving with deliberation in and out.

"Yes," she cried.

With measured movements, he began to fill her again. The molten core of her body tightened around him. His touch seared. Heat flooded her body. She ached for more. She didn't just want him...she needed him. Her body begged for release. Her hips rose to match his thrusts, demanding more. Her arms gripped his shoulders. She leaned her face to the broad blade of his collarbone.

His hands came 'round to cup her backside, and he scooted up on his knees to increase his pace. Each thrust demanded more, forcing her to respond in kind. Each plunge seemed to penetrate the essence of her being and pose a question...would she be his? And she answered with her body. Yes.

"I love you," he whispered in her ear as she climaxed.

"I love you," Wendee said, meaning it with every fiber of her being.

****

The sky lit and thunder crackled around them. Wendee smelled the ozone that electrified the air. Toby held her tight against his body. With gentle fingers, he pushed her soaked hair back from her brow. Her hands cupped his cheeks as she sat straddled, at ease on his knees while his shoulders and head formed a protective canopy around her. His palm rested against the back of her head, his arm to his elbow ran the length of her spine, while his other hand cupped her ass, holding her in place, moored to him, their union complete.

The feel of him inside her, she climaxed, filled with an even deeper tenderness than while they made love. This connection with another, this feeling of oneness, brought a sob to her lips. How could she walk away?

Yet, she had to. There was no more delaying. She had to go.

Toby kissed her cheek, and then reached to retrieve something. A blanket came across her back, insulating the warmth from their bodies. "Whatever this is, Wendee, I will be here for you."

"You can't," she said, only to have her words cut off from the lump in her throat preventing even syllables from escaping. She tilted her head so her brow rested along the hollow of his shoulder. She tried again. "I can't let you. You don't know…"

He moved his hand, and his thumb reached under her chin, forcing her to look at him.

Lightning danced off the water, reflected in his eyes. Some part of Wendee registered the last place they should be in a storm was on the beach. Yet, there was no place else she would be. With him, she felt safer than at any other point in her life. His silvery eyes glowed in the unearthly light, making her believe everything was possible.

"You can't tell me anything I wouldn't understand." He chuckled. "Come on. Look at me. Tell me. Let me share the burden." His fingers reached around her neck and massaged the tight cords. "You taught me. You released me. Now, let me do the same for you. Let's stop running, together."

She sighed and rested her forehead against his. "I don't know if I can."

He moved back, head cocked to the side while one brow rose.

She couldn't help her smile. "Okay," she said, and drew a big breath. "It's a series of stupid choices from the beginning."

He brushed back her hair. "I doubt that."

"I was training for my CGA." When his brow wrinkled, Wendee elaborated. "Accounting designation."

His eyes widened in the glow from the storm. "You're an accountant?"

"Not yet, but don't sound so surprised."

He chuckled and wrapped his arms tighter. "You're just not what I would have pictured for a numbers gal. I picture a woman with horn-rimmed glasses and shirts that button to the neck. Uptight."

She wriggled her bottom. "I do wear glasses and could wear the clothes—"

He growled and the hand across her ass squeezed. "Clothes?" His eyes dipped to her breasts, squished between their bodies. "Stop evading. No distractions." He held her firm.

She huffed, the seriousness of the discussion

elevated somewhat. The levity peaked and died within a couple of seconds. Wendee appreciated the attempt. Toby made it easier to talk without the heaviness of uncertainty. "At any rate." Her fingers brushed along the stubble of his jawline. "Nan was getting worse and needed a convalescent home. She'd been swindled out of all her money years before by my father...I didn't want...I should have...she wouldn't have wanted me to approach the family... She's prideful, you see."

"Go on."

"Fuck...I needed the money. Roger was bad news. He was well known throughout the city, but I really needed the funds to pay for the care Nan deserved. I was only the bookkeeper, for Christ's sake. I would take care of the legitimate lines of business." She broke off, palms covering her face. "I never went near the organized stuff. Never."

"It's okay," Toby soothed. "Nobody is here to judge. Certainly not me."

Thunder crashed, and a wave rolled across her backside, sending a shiver along her spine. She moved her hands from her cheeks to his and squeezed his face. "I wasn't involved in the organized crime stuff, I swear. But someone was siphoning money. Roger needed a fall guy, and he picked me." She reached around and rubbed her shoulder.

Toby stiffened under her. His hands fisted. "What did he do to you?"

His voice had that menacing air, the same as when he spoke about the rapists of his sister.

Wendee shook her head. "Nothing like that. He tried to shoot me." She giggled nervously. "Obviously he failed."

"What?" Toby jerked, launched her from his lap, grabbed her before she fell, and sat again on the sand, the rain pouring down upon them. "Shot you? That's what that is? Powder burn?"

"Nan had just been admitted to hospital, and he had threatened her. Several bullets flew that night. I ran, got Nan settled the best I could, and then kept going."

"Now he's found you." Toby's voice had assumed a low tenor.

Wendee shook her head. "I thought he had. But this cop—"

"Kingston."

"Yeah. Kingston. Whatever the police want with me can't be good."

While the air pulsed around them, Toby held her. After a prolonged pause, he cupped her cheek. "Let's look at this logically," he said, and then pulled the blanket tighter around her shoulders. "It's not easy, mind. But tell me...what would Roger have to gain involving the cops? In my vast knowledge of people in the habit of avoiding the law, it would seem highly imprudent for him to contact the authorities."

"What else could it be?"

He shook his head, whipping his hair from his brow to clear the rain-soaked hair from his eyes. "Instead of running right away, let's delve a little deeper."

"But, what if—"

"I'm here for the what-if," he said. "Let's do something neither of us is used to..."

"What?" she asked.

"Take a chance."

Chapter Sixteen

The wind picked up as they walked along the shoreline to Eva's house. Wet as they were, Toby didn't feel cold. With an arm draped over Wendee's shoulders, they strolled in silence, comfortable in each other's company.

His hand adjusted so his fingers splayed the base of her skull, and he lightly massaged in time to their step. "Can you tell me…" He let the question hang, uncertain in which order to place the multitude of questions.

She glanced up, eyes blinking rapidly. Rivulets of rain ran across her cheeks.

The hollow at the base of her throat contracted before a sigh and a nod communicated back to him. "Yes." With the storm in full rage, he bent close to hear and be heard over nature's chaos. "Is it Cavanaugh or Miller?" he asked.

She lowered her gaze and chuckled lightly. "Neither, and both, really."

He shook his head, his fingers ceasing their kneading to flop back in to place, following the slope of her arm. "It's okay if you don't—"

"No, no." She lifted a hand to brush along the front of his mangled shirt, pulling it closed where the buttons were not missing. "It's okay, really. My legal name is Hamsworth."

Toby squinted against the stream of water

obscuring his vision. He shook his head, repeating the name in his mind.

"Long story short, my parents were never officially"—Wendee raised her fingers in an air quote—"married. But I was given the Hamsworth surname. Miller is Nan's married name, and Cavanaugh her maiden, and the one my mom preferred and used."

"She didn't like your granddad?"

"I didn't know him, but Nan loved him dearly. But, you see, Cavanaugh is a big name in banking. Full of money and prestige. There was a time when Mom felt entitled to some of that and decided if she carried the name, some of that wealth would strike her too. Not that she didn't have money, she just...I don't know really, to be honest."

Toby nodded. Motivation for other people's actions was a hard nut to crack.

"I think some of that seeking prestige is what led her and my father together. They had that search for the limelight in common. Dad was a budding sports star—hockey, to be specific—one year in the NHL."

"I like hockey," Toby said with a bow of his head.

"I used to," Wendee replied, dryly. "He was apparently best new draft overall, and all of that. Met my mom the first year in, and she fell pregnant with me. But, injury after injury saw him cut. He traded on his name for a while thereafter. Nan did her best to help him out with all of her old social connections from the Cavanaugh banking side of the family, and that seemed to do the trick for a period of time, until it didn't. Enough was never enough. Then Mom got sick, and Dad was too busy for a kid and a woman he didn't feel connected to in any way."

"That can't be true," Toby interjected.

Wendee squeezed both arms around his middle. "Yes, indeed it is. He told me so. Said he had too much living to do to be saddled with an albatross. When Mom died, he bargained with Nan, who paid him a huge sum of her inheritance to keep me when he threatened to leave me to the foster system. Like Nan would have ever let that happen." Wendee snorted and shook her head. "None of that was true, of course, I had plenty of extended family who would have stepped up, but really all he wanted was a piece of the Cavanaugh fortune. Nan said she'd have joyfully gone bankrupt."

"She sounds like an outstanding woman."

"She sure was." Wendee paused, staring ahead, wondering what her father even looked like now. Did she care? "So, he took off to enjoy his life, and we never heard from him again. Couple of decades now."

A series of shivers coursed under Toby's fingers. "You're cold. Let's get you home and warm again."

"No, it's not that," she said with a shake of her head. "I just wish—oh my God."

Toby followed her gaze to the squad car parked on the road out front of Eva's house. "What do you want to do?"

She turned in his arms. "You can't be here."

"The hell I can't. I'm not leaving you."

"What if they want to question you?" Her voice was rising along with the scream of the wind. "What will you do? You jeopardize everything by staying here. I can't have that for you, Toby. I can't be responsible for that."

"You're not responsible. I am," he said with a firm shake of his head. "Whatever happens is bound to happen at some point. I want to be here for you. I need to be here for you." He gripped her shoulders. "Can you understand? I can't leave you. You are not alone. You have Eva...you have me."

The fingers that rose to cover her lips trembled. Her wide, amber eyes seemed to consume her face as she rose up to kiss him. "Okay."

He linked his fingers with hers, and they opened the gate and approached the front door.

****

Toby nodded encouragement when her hand wrapped around the door handle. "Deep breath," he said as she swung the door wide and stepped through.

The door stopped part-way, blocked by a broad shoulders in navy blue. An officer in full uniform moved aside as they entered. Notepad in hand, he scrutinized their appearance from head to toe. His gaze seemed to linger on the rips of Toby's ill put-together shirt.

A female officer stood next to a sobbing blonde woman, whose hands flanked her cheeks as she rocked back and forth on her heels.

Starting with an audible, "Thank God," the slender woman wobbled toward Wendee, who dropped his hand and raced to meet Eva and wrap her cousin in a tight embrace.

"I'm so sorry." Wendee patted the slender woman's back. "I am so sorry."

"You know?" Eva lifted her face from Wendee's shoulder. "How could you know?"

Wendee's face became a mask of confusion. "Officer Kingston was at the hotel earlier."

"Kingston?" the male officer interjected, lifting his

161

notepad. "Why was he looking for you? We only have Evangeline Vincent as the next of kin to be notified in the case of an emergency, and I don't know an officer Kingston."

"Yes, Kingston," Eva said with a nod. "But that was for—"

"Next of kin?" Wendee stepped back from Eva and turned to the officer.

Eva laid a hand on Wendee's shoulder. "It's Trip," she choked and sobbed again. She pulled tissue from the box on the table under a large print. She blew her nose noisily. "There's been a terrible car accident up in San Francisco."

"Trip?" the female officer questioned.

"Travis is my brother's name," Eva said with impatience. "Trip is the name his family and fans know him by."

"Excuse me, please." The officer seemed to realize she was being inappropriate.

Toby didn't know whether to stay or go. Obviously, this had nothing to do with Wendee, but the question remained, what would she do when Kingston did find her? Toby didn't want to leave her. Couldn't.

"He's in the hospital." Eva lowered her head to Wendee's shoulder. "They won't tell me any more than that. I don't know if he was alone. If Kurt was with him. Nothing."

Wendee drew Eva close and stroked her cousin's hair.

To Toby's eyes, she grew inches as she maneuvered around to face the police. "What can you tell us?"

The officers shared a look before continuing. The

female officer began reading from her notepad. "Mr. Vincent and Mr. Davidson—"

"Kurt *was* with him," Eva said.

The officer nodded. "I'm sorry. Both Vincent and Davidson ran off a cliff about three hours ago and were airlifted to a hospital. Mr. Davidson was pronounced dead at the scene—"

"Ohmygod, Kurt." Eva stood back from Wendee's embrace and swiped her palms across her eyes. She shook her head and straightened her shoulders. She walked to the hall closet and gathered her coat and purse. "I have to go…now."

"I'll come with you." Wendee glanced down, noticing for the first time she was dripping all over the hardwood floor. "I'll just run upstairs and grab a change."

Then both women took note of Toby standing there. "Toby, I—"

"No, Wendee, you stay," Eva said with a firmness of tone her face didn't confirm. "You need to be here." She reached under the tissue box, drew out a folded piece of paper, and handed it to Wendee. "You take care of this, and I will be back as soon as I can."

****

An hour later, the empty house weighed upon her shoulders, adding to the bricks lining her stomach as she stared at the paper crumpled in her hand. She had changed while the thunder crashed, yet she couldn't bring herself to unfold the paper.

Toby stepped forward and sandwiched her hand between his.

"She knows," Wendee whispered, turning her gaze up to meet Toby's. "What could she think?"

He shook his head. "She loves you."

Tears gathered in her eyes. Poor Eva, first to find out she had harbored a woman on the run, and then her brother… "I'm scared."

"I know," he said, and pulled her close.

Wendee felt surrounded by his warmth. She breathed in his scent. He smelled of the beach and security. Knowing that Trip's life hung in the balance in some hospital in San Francisco and what Eva must be going through trying to get to him in time, never mind the strength of the man standing before her, put her problems in perspective. Whatever the police wanted, she could face it. Finally, she realized she was not alone.

With trembling fingers, she unfolded the paper. Two scraps of newsprint floated out from the seam. Toby grabbed them before they spread across the floor.

"What is it?" she asked when he held them both by a corner.

"Newspaper articles. Oops, sorry, one's a notice."

"Let me see," she said, and reached for the larger of the two. She read the headline, and then leaned against the wall behind her to balance.

Toby grabbed her by the elbow. "It's okay. Let's sit down."

"It can't be."

Toby scanned the page, his head nodding. "Seems like it can."

Relief bubbled up over the lump in her throat and emerged closer to a bark than laughter. "Should I wait for him to come back, or go find him?"

Toby drew her to him then, with his hands on her shoulders, held her from him. "Read the note from

Eva."

Wendee smoothed the creases from the page. She coughed.

"*You should have told me.*"

Wendee glanced up at Toby. "She's right. I should have told her."

"Read on," he encouraged.

"*Don't go into this alone. Kingston explained everything to me, figuring you may try to avoid him or run again. You need a good lawyer, and I have a contact in Minnesota who can set you up.*"

Wendee wiped the tears that filled her eyes. "Eva knows everyone."

"You know you can trust her. She obviously has your back."

"I should never have doubted," Wendee said. "I can't believe it. All this time, they've been looking for me as a witness, not a suspect."

Toby pulled the newspaper article from her fingers and read:

"*A Dozen Members of Western States Brotherhood Organization Indicted for Conspiracy to Distribute Methamphetamine, Money Laundering, and Related Charges.*"

He shook his head, hunkered down next to her, and continued reading.

Twelve members of the drug trafficking organization, including local businessman, Roger Brodie, charged. The indictment is the result of a three-year investigation."

Toby whistled. "Wow, seems everyone from Homeland Security to the Drug Enforcement Agency were involved. They're looking for you, because you have the missing piece of the puzzle."

"The money trail."

They sat quiet for a long while. Then, Toby broke the silence. "What will you do?"

"The right thing," she said, cupping his cheeks. "Finally, the right thing. Make a sound decision." Then she wrapped her arms about Toby's neck. "But you can't come with me. I won't chance it. I won't have you being found inadvertently." When he shook his head, his light eyes hardening to steel, she held his face firmly. "It's too dangerous."

"I don't care—"

"I do," she said, her voice sounding strained. "What you did, you did for love, and it was an accident."

When he shook his head, she nodded. "Yes. Yes, it was. I don't care what you say. You could never have known the outcome. So you boxed and won a couple of championships. There's more to this story. More you were too young to fathom and—"

"I wasn't there for my own family," he said, blinking back the moisture that filled his eyes and threatened to spill. "Let me be there for you."

"Be here for me when I come back."

Chapter Seventeen

Wendee ran through the arrival doors and gripped Eva close. "Are they here?"

"Not yet," Eva said, turning toward the baggage area. "They're arriving by boat."

"Boat? Are you kidding me? Jeez, I wouldn't have the patience." The women turned and walked shoulder-to-shoulder down the wide corridor, wading between the throngs of people, passengers and visitors alike. "Does he know?"

"I can't see how," Eva responded, tossing a look across to Wendee. "I've seen him quite a bit, but he's only ever interested in you and how things were progressing in Minnesota." Eva poked her with a gentle elbow. "You're a lucky girl."

So much had happened in the six weeks since she flew back to the Midwest. Her testimony on record, the trial would be set for the following year. She wasn't done yet, but she was done with Minnesota for now. Eva's brother, Trip, had survived the car wreck physically, but mentally, she wasn't so sure. Eva had convinced him to convalesce with her.

"He's a handful, but he needs someplace stable now. The loss of Kurt..." She trailed off and swiped a finger under her eye.

Wendee reached across her cousin's back to squeeze her while they walked toward the exit.

"Anyway," Eva said, taking a shuddered breath. "You two are quite the pair. His family had no way to find him. They didn't know he even survived the storm that sank the boat where he stowed away. That they continued with the appeal process regardless is incredible. With him assumed dead, the courts consented."

"He doesn't know any of this. Doesn't even know the boat sank," Wendee said, with a shake of her head. "Such strange circumstances that brings people together."

They retrieved her bags and made their way toward the exit. Both women had agreed not to relay the news to Toby until they had all the facts, and then Eva made arrangements for his family to come to the island.

"You're telling me." Eva reached into her bag for her key fob and double-clicked it to open the car doors. She started the ignition, and the air conditioning grazed across their skin in a gentle breeze. "Been as hot as the hinges of Hell here this last month."

Wendee clipped her seatbelt. "Go on, tell me everything."

"Toby was both a wrestler and boxer in high school. Even had a scholarship."

"He didn't tell me." Wendee glanced down at her hands. So much she didn't yet know about Tobias MacPherson. So much she wanted to know, and thanks to her cousin and her multitude of connections, she and Toby would have all the time in the world to get to know each other.

"After the…situation with his sister." Eva reached across and took Wendee's hand.

"And the trio got off," Wendee added.

"Toby went for them, but he was goaded on. Seems he called them out in front of their families. Stood on the lawn and yelled at them. Asked them how they could live with themselves. One of the boys had also been on the wrestling team, and he and Toby had been competitors for the same scholarship."

Eva stopped to pay the parking fee. "They claimed to be such church-going people." Eva seemed to choke on the words. "How they could attend church knowing what their sons had done? When no one came out and Toby had apparently exhausted himself, he walked away."

"He walked away?" Eva had told her this previously, but the whole situation struck Wendee each time she heard it. "He's convinced himself he was a killer."

"The boy followed, and that's when the real fight happened," Eva continued. "Toby's one big boy."

Wendee smiled, envisioning his strong arms around her. "He is."

"Well, you know what happened." Eva slipped the car into gear and maneuvered out of airport parking onto the freeway.

"But Toby stood trial. He went to jail."

"Yes. He wasn't incarcerated long. About the time the family of the other boy came forward, Toby had already escaped." Eva rolled up the window to let the air conditioning do its job. "Had he even waited another month, he would have been a free man."

"Freedom," Wendee whispered. How much the word meant to her, and to Toby.

"A witness came forward, backing up that Toby didn't incite it and only defended himself. However much he may have provoked it, going to the family's home. In the end, his tirade proved the point, and atonement was made."

"Sometimes justice does pay off."

"Sometimes," Eva agreed, maneuvering the sports car toward San Diego and home.

****

"I wouldn't call this a stroll. More of a brisk walk," Toby said, pulling Wendee to him. He smelled her hair and ran his nose along the side of her head, by her ear, and dipped to plant a kiss in the hollow of her neck. "You smell so good."

"I'm eager to give you a surprise," she said, her heart hammering against her ribcage. Maybe she should have just told him. But truth be told, she didn't know how to tell him coherently. There was just so much. He had to see them. He had to know.

"What could be more of a surprise than you being here?" He lifted his head, his silvery eyes crinkled with the same smile that brought out his dimples. "You should have told me. Eva could have told me you were coming home today."

Wendee shrugged. "Didn't wanna. I already told you I wanted to surprise you."

"Okay, then enough surprises," he said, his voice lowering to a throaty promise of things to come. "Let me do for you."

Her heart skipped a beat. "Oh, you do for me all right."

His hand slipped lower on her back. "How I love that glint in your eye."

"Come on." She pulled on his hand. "I see it up ahead."

"The sailboat?"

The breath seemed to leave her body. "Yes," was all she was able to mutter as they walked down to the small pier. Then she added, "Because I love you."

He stopped. "You love me?"

"I do." She smiled up at him, and then reached to kiss his lips. "Come on."

"Wendee. I want to be with you, always." He cupped her cheek then pushed her cropped hair behind an ear. "I love you."

"I know."

****

Toby's fingers laced with Wendee's and tightened as they approached the boat. An older woman was being helped down the gangplank. Was this a new sailing excursion? He'd rather be alone with Wendee on the houseboat. Their houseboat, now. Yet, she continued to pull him forward.

Up ahead, he watched as a man followed the woman off the boat. Tall, like Toby, when the stranger removed his ball cap, his shiny bald dome reflected the evening sun, giving him a glow. Toby watched as the man straightened and rolled his shoulders, running a hand across his forehead before replacing his cap. The movement caught Toby as familiar. A quick flick of his head from side to side, as though adjusting his neck from a crick, made Toby stop in his tracks.

His gaze trailed to the older woman. Plump, but not fat, her cheeks drew up like an apple doll. Apple doll. "Ma." The word hissed out, and his knees seemed to turn to water. He dropped Wendee's hand.

The woman's head came up, though he knew there was no way she could have heard him from this distance. Yet, her gaze locked with his, and he could see the familiar glint, a mirror of his own.

She swayed, and the man behind her caught her elbow.

Toby's body worked instinctively, allowing his mind to catch up, and he had begun to approach the people on the deck. He stopped a mere foot from them, glancing from one to the other. "Ma? Bob?"

"Son."

If you enjoyed *From the Front Desk*, turn the page for a preview of *For a Song,* Book Three in the Gentle Surf Series.

For a Song

by

Lori Power

The Gentle Surf, Book Three

Chapter One

Trip Vincent scrubbed his palms across his eyes. They itched and burned from the dry, recycled air. The heat and odor of the mass of accumulated bodies crowding the courtroom caused acid to roll in his stomach.

"All stand, for the Right Honorable…"

Trip's hands fell to the tabletop and his head snapped around to focus on the rear of the dais. The remains of the bailiff's announcement were lost in the shuffle of people rising from the packed benches, their eagerness like a pheromone scent. A hush descended the throng, then a heavy cough echoed off the domed ceiling. Trip didn't need to hear the rest. He knew the routine well by this point of the trial.

A moment later, a stern-faced judge swept into the room from the alcove to the back of the raised stand. Cloaked in the traditional legislative black robes and white cravat, he looked every inch the part with his wavy gray hair and neat beard as he swept across the landing with a regal air. He took a half second to regard the courtroom with small, deep-set penetrating eyes before taking his seat. His robes billowed up like a cloud before settling around him while he shuffled some paper on his desk. His presence sucked the oxygen from the room. Then he nodded and everyone obediently resumed their seats.

Everyone, except Trip Vincent and his lawyer.

Trip's long fingers splayed across the surface of the polished wooden table while he forced his knees to lock so he too could stand still without shaking. A flutter twitched under his right eye and he squeezed both shut. None of this mattered. His hands balled into fists. Whatever the verdict, the punishment would never bring his best friend back. To the marrow of his bones he knew that. Trip opened his eyes to face the magistrate, willing himself to wake from the nightmare.

The judge nodded at Trip's lawyer. "Be seated," he said. His crisp voice carried across the room, each syllable struck like a hammer in expectation of what was to come.

Trip stared at the judge, whose prominent feature, a pronounced lower jaw, seemed to amplify his words. The trim goatee did little to soften the effect. Yet Trip remained grateful that today would mark the end of the fiasco. Months of media frenzy, prosecution via the social mob, the brunt of bad jokes on late night television, combined with trial preparation had long since zapped Trip's zest for this life. There seemed no safe harbor for him any longer. No place to hide, nowhere to escape, and he lacked the courage to end it on his own.

His ears were deaf to the preamble of whatever the judge said. Trip ground his teeth and tried to concentrate, to dig himself out of the void of black despair. Then his shoulder slumped, defeated before he even began. What was the use? Every day he relived the night his world tipped on its axis and all that was good died. Didn't anyone in this room realize he'd gladly welcome the cell if it would only allow him to escape the jail of his own memories—the iron smell of gushing blood, the gurgling sounds of the last rattled breaths, the vacant look that settles on the eyes that are alive no more.

Trip balanced on the edge of his chair, his foot nervously bouncing up and down. On his right, his lawyer, ever the cool cucumber, relaxed into position with an elbow loosely hanging from the back of his perch. Every so often, his nose, bulbous as a turnip, the same purple hue to match, would flare its nostrils and Trip knew he should pay attention. An accompaniment to the lawyer's lead, he would nod his head in agreement to the justice being met out. Did that mean they were winning? How could they? Everything was lost. Was the judge speaking English? Trip couldn't understand a word.

This case warranted no jury, his lawyer had explained months ago. His fate instead—his future— remained entirely in the hands of a judge—a man whose name Trip could not recall and referred to him as "Jaws" whenever he recounted the events of the day to his sister during their daily debriefs.

Kurt Nathanial Davidson was the only name on his mind. A name capitalized in every newspaper headline today. A name etched on a gravestone Trip had not had the audacity to see.

With a flap of his fingers, the judge focused on Trip. "Would the defendant Travis Michael Vincent rise."

Trip understood the motion and obeyed, forcing his body to unfold from the seat. His heart slammed against his ribs and the urge to urinate almost overcame him. Then the pat on his shoulder brought him back from the brink. "Ah, what?" Trip asked, turning his head to face his lawyer.

The lawyer's face split wide with a grin, revealing chemically altered, unnaturally white teeth, a stark contrast to the color of his nose. "We did it. You're all but free."

"What... How?"

"Come on," the lawyer with his linebacker build, tugged Trip by the elbow to propel him forward. "Let's get out while we can. I've called for the car."

"How?"

"How?" His lawyer turned, black eyes almost shark-like stared through Trip, making his insides quake further, unable to comprehend any kind of good news. "Because I'm the best lawyer money can buy," he returned in a loud whisper next to his ear.

"But..."

"Never mind that now," he said, propelling Trip through the crowd. "We'll review the next steps in the car. We're close to the finish line now."

The best money could buy. Trip's focus fell to his business manager, Arnold Switzer, who sat unmoving in the front aisle. With a slight pivot of his head, he gazed in Trip's direction as though on autopilot, when they scooted past. The corners of Arnold's lips lifted but fell far short of a smile. The crease between his eyes deepened and his stare remained unfocused.

Trip ached to reach out to Arnold and ask him what this all meant. But Arnold looked as mystified as Trip felt.

He shouldn't have forbidden his sister Eva from attending. Perhaps a friendly face—someone who actually loved him would have helped make sense out of all the confusion. But he couldn't take the disappointment he knew she'd try to hide.

When had life become so chaotic? Certainly long before the trial.

Bailiffs held the heavy mahogany doors while they exited. Flash bulbs assaulted his vision, the flare rendering him momentarily blind. Still he strode on, dimly following his lawyer through the gathering crowd.

On the periphery, jeers and cat-calls resonated off the stylized stone walls. He opened his mouth to speak, but what could he say? He clamped his lips together. There was no easy comeback. Easy had died. He couldn't even muster enough anger at the insults to make an impression. Even the teenaged girl who threw broken pieces of his band's record at him couldn't get a rise. Former fans ripped his face from magazines and tossed the crumpled pages at his feet while he walked on. And everywhere smart phones recorded the scene to spread across the multitude of social media channels. He continued to be media sensation. Now, for all the wrong reasons.

He thought he had long since given up paying attention to the armchair juries. They weren't saying anything he didn't already know. He, Trip Vincent, had killed the lifeblood of the band, their soul, and future, *and* he had gotten away with it. What they didn't know was he had done this long before the crash that took Kurt's life.

Suddenly, the red-tipped claws of an attacker pushed against his chest and he teetered back a pace.

"Coward," Janet Davidson screamed directly in his face, spittle spraying across his nose.

Her eyes bulged and with each gasping breath, her face grew near to purple under a layer of cement-like foundation. So incensed, her bloodshot eyes glowed in the florescent lights. With her nose mere inches away from his, he noted the eyeliner build-up in the corners. "Community service! Who did you bribe?" Her claws tightened and he felt the pointed tips rake across his chest.

Retaining her grip on his shirt, she whirled to address the media, her other arm flung out in accusation. She was their queen of the moment. Her theatrics well documented in the past had grown to epic proportions with the case. "My brother's dead from this deadbeat druggy. My brother's dead and he…" Janet released him then and an accusatory finger shot up to his chin. "Gets community service—"

"Enough, miss." A security officer approached, his wide shoulders parted the crowd. Zigzagging, he pushed his way to stand between Trip and his former lover, who also happened to be the over-indulged sister of his now dead partner. "Come, make room." The squat security officer took her by her elbow to maneuver her away from the mob.

A cacophony of profanities chorused her outburst from the throng pushing against the guards lining the exit. The crush of the horde prevented Trip from even focusing on his shoes as he walked. Looking everywhere, but nowhere, he tried to avert his gaze from everyone. Then he couldn't help himself, his eyes locked on another's. Perhaps it was the lack of movement, her calm in the sea of chaos, that caught his attention. He staggered forward, propelled by his handlers, but there seemed nowhere to go. A woman, petite, dressed in plain faded jeans and a white T-shirt, should never have even been visible in this crowd. But she was. Her eyes, round and luminous against the raven spikes of her hair, held him. In a moment filled with hatred and loathing, she gave him a feeling of peace. An emotion he had no right to sense. Yet, more than sympathy etched her expression. With a slight tilt of her head, she seemed to reach across the distance and tell him she understood where and how things had gone so very wrong.

"C'mon Trip." His lawyer tugged his sleeve to keep him moving. "We'll work out the details later."

Trip turned to nod to the lawyer and laid his palm on his chest where Janet's hand had provided the only warmth his body had felt in days. There was sure to be a bruise. Then he glanced back over his shoulder to where the woman had stood.

She was gone. And with her, his moment of grace.

He swung around, searching for her, grasping to *feel* again. Something—anything. But pandemonium surrounded him.

On his heels, Janet pulled against the restraint of the guard. "My brother's dead!" she screamed. "Dead."

Trip dropped his arm and stashed his hands in his pockets, then hung his head. He couldn't make eye contact. Not with Janet. Not with anyone. Not anymore. He couldn't face his reflection in the glass doors.

"Murderer—"

Trip didn't deserve freedom. He'd failed his friend.

In reality, he deserved the heckles. Because of his action, his lack of forethought, he had killed his best friend—his only friend. And he did it on purpose.

"Shameful—" The sentence sliced into silence

when the car door slammed blocking the sounds of protesters. Eggs splashed off the windows. The yolks a thick smudge, the wrong color, but reminiscent none-the-less of the texture of Kurt's blood when it splattered over the passenger window where it impaled his chest.

Trip slumped down in the seat, pushed his shirtsleeves up to his elbows, and covered his eyes with his palms to hide despite being shrouded by the tinted windows.

Arnold slipped in on the other side. Trip expected the same silence he'd received from Arnold these past two months. Instead, *Iron Clad's* manager miraculously, in the last few moments, seemed to shake off the black cloud and patted Trips knee in his old familial way. "We'll start fresh."

Trip splayed his fingers wide to searched Arnold's face for signs of lunacy.

"Excuse me," he croaked, clamping his jaw to ward off further words.

Only the smallest shadow of sorrow seemed to hang within Arnold's gaze, the crease of his forehead lessened above the bushy brows when he smiled back. "You were always *meant* to be the lead singer. The industry is swamped with songs for the picking. We'll get you a new songbook and we're off to the races, my boy. Capitalize on all this frenzy. Your name is magic. Back on top in no time at all."

Was he serious? Just like that? Trip lowered his hands and braced his fingers across the bridge of his nose. Grace? What was he thinking? An imagined response. There would never be any grace for him—not ever. Yet, he looked back toward the courthouse, wondering about the woman.

He flinched as hands slapped against the panes of the smoky windows, winced as though he were being whipped. They—the horde and Janet—were right, of course. He merited no compassion. Community service being woefully lame compared to the punishment he deserved. But then he looked back at Arnold, and managed a nod. Could he really be so cowardly...because he was relieved.

A word about the author...

Attracted to the deeper meaning of roots, family, and community within each of us, Lori uses these philosophies to form the foundation of the characters in all of her writing.

In business, as in life, Lori has discovered a truism: everyone has a great story to tell. All you need to do is listen. Over the years, with all the people Lori has met previously and daily, both professionally and personally, with an ear to the ground, readers can often find these "characters" fictionalized in stories.

Collaboration is important to improving one's craft, and therefore Lori is an active member of the TransCanada Romance Writers, Romance Writers of America, The Alberta Romance Writers Association, and belongs to both a critiquing group and a beta reading weekly group.

In all things, remember...life is a journey—enjoy the adventure!

Thank you for purchasing
this publication of The Wild Rose Press, Inc.

If you enjoyed the story, we would appreciate your
letting others know by leaving a review.

For other wonderful stories,
please visit our on-line bookstore at
www.thewildrosepress.com.

For questions or more information
contact us at
info@thewildrosepress.com.

The Wild Rose Press, Inc.
www.thewildrosepress.com

Stay current with The Wild Rose Press, Inc.

Like us on Facebook

https://www.facebook.com/TheWildRosePress

And Follow us on Twitter
https://twitter.com/WildRosePress